# DEVIL IN GOLD

*A Billionaire Romance*

SHANNA HANDEL

# Beauties & Billionaires

## WELCOME

Devil in Gold: A Billionaire Romance (Beauties and Billionaires)

By Shanna Handel

Copyright © 2022 Shanna Handel

All rights reserved.

Artwork by Pop Kitty Design

Editing by Jane Beyer

Proofread by Julie Barney

# SYNOPSIS

Devil in Gold: A Billionaire Romance

Shanna Handel

***If he's the Devil, I think I'm losing my religion***

The good girl preacher's daughter selling her virginity to the bad boy billionaire?

He can see I'm contemplating it. He takes the opportunity to lean over and whisper a number in my ear. A very big number. With a lot of zeros.

It's enough money to change my father's life. But using my body to pay for it? If my father ever found out, I wouldn't need the money because the reverend would keel over and die.

I eye Preston.

He was the bad boy of our small town. Always sneaking off into the woods with girls and whiskey. My dad called him the Devil.

Now he's a billionaire and part of the elusive Bachman family. Even more demanding and gorgeous than when he left. Ten years ago he set my body on fire with his tongue. Made me tremble with the stroke of his hand.

He may have left my virginity intact. But I've never been that close to heaven.

He has an indecent proposal for me. Something he wants in exchange for something I desperately need.

*I think I might be about to make a deal with the Devil.*

## 1

# J ules

Carrie Underwood belts *How Great Thou Art* through my kitchen, making me jump, startled, and fling cookie dough onto the counter. *Thanks for the new ringtone, Dad.* He must have gotten into my phone again. Tossing the tray of cookies into the oven, I wipe my hands on the front of my apron and slip my phone from the pocket.

"Hello?"

An automated voice with a snooty tone comes over the line. "Please note this call is an attempt from the Rosebery Medical Center to collect a debt."

I bury my head in my still sticky hand and groan. "Not another one." My dad's unpaid bills are stacking up faster than I can get them plugged into my debt spreadsheet.

I hang up and start digging around in the kitchen drawers for the checkbook. I swear I left it in the one on the right with the neatly lined up pens and Post-it Notes.

"Dad? Did you move the checkbook?" I restack already neatly placed envelopes in their shallow basket and close the drawer.

No answer.

I untie the apron, hanging it up neatly on its hook inside the tidy pantry. A place for everything and everything in its place. I leave the kitchen, peeking in our tiny, overflowing bookshelved living room. "Dad? You in here?"

Hmm...not in his reading chair where he usually is. I search the house. It only takes a minute to comb our two-bed one-bath shoebox. He's not here.

*Shoot.*

Where's he gone off to now?

Two weeks ago I found him rumbling around in the church basement, looking for hymnals that he'd sold on eBay last year. Lately he's been having more of these spacy episodes, wandering around town, forgetting appointments.

I'm not sure how much longer I'll be able to hide his declining health from his congregation. He can still holler out a moving sermon. His flock loves their shepherd.

And without his meager pastoral income...

We're totally screwed.

Maybe Dad went for a walk. He'll be back any second. I busy myself with the only thing in this world that can pull me out of a funk...

A favorite book.

I grab my worn copy of *Pride and Prejudice* from the counter. I've left it open and the poor, darling book is doing the full splits to mark my place—I know, I'm a monster.

The timer dings just when I'm at the part where Darcy basically says Elizabeth is cute, but not cute enough for him. I've read the book a hundred times but still, my blood boils for her. Reluctantly, I close the book, this time making a tiny respectful dog-ear at the top of the page to mark my place and leave it on the counter.

I pull the pan from the oven and do the trick Ms. Clancy down the street showed me, where you put a glass around the hot cookies and use it to make them into perfect circles. The result is golden-brown, magazine-worthy treats.

I make a fresh pot of coffee and prepare for a stress eating marathon.

Our financial future is not looking promising. Apparently, my dad didn't believe in disability insurance, or a 401k. I have savings from my last job as an online fashion influencer—wow, that was a different life—but it's quickly dwindling.

Dad's not back yet.

Where is he? I'm surprised the scent of baking didn't bring him to the kitchen.

I go to the only place I've not yet checked. The hall closet. He can't be in there.

*Can he?*

Last night I heard crazy banging noises coming from the wall my room shares with the closet. Too enthralled with my *Desperate Housewives of Vegas* marathon to get out of bed, I called out to him to see what he was doing. He popped his head in my room and said he was just hammering in some new coat hooks.

I didn't think much of it till now. Come to think of it, I never saw him this morning. Oh my gosh, what if he passed out in there or something last night?

I open the door to the closet. A cloud of drywall dust comes billowing out, making me cover my mouth and cough. "What in the world?" I wave my hand in front of me, clearing the air.

"Dad. What have you been up to?" I ask myself.

An eerie feeling comes over me. Little prickles dance down my spine as I step into the closet.

There's a pile of chunks of drywall. No new coat hooks. It looks like Dad was doing a little late night demo work?

There's a massive hole in the back wall of the closet. *What's that?* I move closer, inspecting a large, long package-looking thing wrapped in something dark that's nestled in the wall. I step closer, holding my phone's flashlight up to get a better look.

The thing is wrapped in black plastic, circles of duct tape wrapped around it every few feet.

The shape and size of the parcel looks a hell of a lot like a...

*Dead body?*

White heat washes over my face. *Jules, don't let your imagination get the best of you.* I set my phone down on the floor, flashlight up. I reach into the hole, wrapping my arms around the object. The plastic feels cold; whatever is inside feels stiff yet yields slightly. It's heavy. I tug it, bringing it halfway out of the hole.

This really feels a lot like what I would imagine a dead body would feel like...

With a shaking hand, I press against the top. It's round and smooth and the right size to be a human skull. It feels a hell of a lot like the top of a head.

It. Is. A. Head.

*This. Is. A. Body.*

Inside our closet. It has to be. What else could it be?

The white heat turns to ice, a snowball of sickness forming in my gut.

*Dad—what have you done?*

There's a knock on the front door. Three business-like raps that startle me right out of my skin. I give a yelp, letting go of the thing. It lands all cockeyed, leaning against what's left of the drywall, kind of half sitting against the closet wall.

"Coming!" My voice is high, strained. I hop out of the closet, brushing drywall dust from my black cropped tee and jeans.

I peek in the hall mirror, expecting my red hair to be standing on end from my fright, but it looks fine. I've grown it past my shoulders, finally embracing my natural curls. I pinch my cheeks, trying to bring some color to my face.

I look like I've just seen a ghost.

Maybe I dreamed the whole thing.

There's a loud thump from the hall closet. I strain my neck, looking for what made the sound.

*Oh, shoot!*

The body-like package has fallen over. It's now laid out on the floor, halfway hanging out of the closet into the hallway.

Three more knocks.

I press my back against the door like my visitor is going to bust up in my house yelling, "Hey Jules, you got any dead bodies in here!?" and I have to stop them.

Another knock.

A deep voice I don't recognize calls out, "Anyone home? Reverend Verduce?"

This isn't really happening. I'm not about to hide a body from a stranger at my front door.

But I am...

I'll just open the door a crack, slip out, and close it real fast.

*One...two...three...*

I open the door a tiny bit and try to push my way through while quickly pulling the door closed behind me. I trip my way out onto the stoop, one hand flying around in the air trying to regain my balance as the other pulls the door shut behind me. I'm fully expecting to fall on my face.

"Oh!" A set of strong arms catches me.

*Wasn't expecting that...*

I stare up into the most gorgeous set of eyes. Familiar eyes. Sexy, make you daydream about them, eyes.

It's been over a decade, but I haven't forgotten those blue-green eyes.

*This...*is Preston.

A decade ago we shared one night together. It started with a life-or-death situation and ended with his tongue in my mouth and his hand up my cheer skirt. Now, he's Preston Bachman, a billionaire and a member of an elusive brotherhood that runs New York City from behind closed doors.

His dad passed away not too long ago. I guess he's here to deal with his father's stuff. I'd assumed he would send someone to do the work. I'm sure Preston has "people" for that kind of thing.

I take him in as I steady myself.

He looks good. Really, really good. His chest and shoulders have filled out more—didn't think that was possible—and he's hung up his ball cap and ripped jeans for an expensive-looking city haircut and casual business attire. There's a light five-o'clock shadow running over his square jaw.

Why do men always look better with age? Am I right?

"Hey. Preston." I tug myself from his arms, backing up against the door. The clean scent of his cologne lingers around me. "Long time no see."

"Jules Verduce." He gives me that cocky, devilish grin that always hits me right in my core. His gaze travels over my body. "Damn. I wasn't expecting you to be here."

"I wasn't expecting to see you either." Like, ever again. Gracious, the man hated this town. "I'm sorry about your father."

I can't believe Preston is here, standing on my doorstep after all this time. He runs a hand through his golden hair, leaving it standing on end. *Sexily disheveled.* I try not to stare at him as he slips his hand in the pocket of his perfectly tailored pants.

*Gah*—even the way he does *that* is sexy.

*No wonder I never got over that night...*

"When I asked who to see about selling my old man's place they gave me your address, but I just assumed I'd be meeting your dad," he says.

"Well," I shrug with a smile. "Surprise! It's me."

"What *are* you doing here?" His brow furrows like a sex god as he stares at me. "Last I'd heard you had some fancy job and apartment in the city. Something with fashion?"

"Ah, I've had some life changes. My dad needed me and...well, when life throws you lemons..."

*You move back home and rot until you die.*

"Oh. Gotcha." He doesn't pry. "How long have you been back?"

"Two years. And thirty-three days and about oh, five hours. But who's counting?" I give a grossly dorky laugh.

"Wow. That long, huh?" He grins at me and I can feel it all the way down in my toes.

I can't tear my eyes from him. His flawless skin is golden from his hours in the sun—I remember he loved to surf.

"Jules?" He tosses me a curious look.

*Huh?*

Was I staring? Do I need to wipe drool from the corner of my mouth? "Sorry. I missed whatever you just said."

His already deep voice drops an octave as he goes into business mode. "I was saying once I get the place packed up, can we get it listed as soon as possible? I'd love the listing to hit the MLS before I head back to the city."

Of course he wants to wash his hands of the place as quickly as he can. What would a successful, hot, charming guy want with this sleepy town? Still, it stings.

His slight to the town makes delivering the bad news a little easier.

He's stuck with that place. I tell him the hard truth. "Your father signed a contract when he bought the house. It can't actually be sold, like to the public, or listed. It can only be transferred to a new Cedar Creek resident. And the Elders of the town have to approve the transfer."

"Alright. I'm emailing my agent now." He's pulling out a really expensive-looking phone with a lot of buttons, his fingertips flying across the screen. "Let's do that. Isn't there a waitlist? I remember my dad saying he waited six months to get this place."

Time to be the bearer of *really* bad news.

"Uh, maybe don't send that email just yet?"

"Why?" He looks up from the screen.

"Your father bought it over a decade ago, when Cedar Creek was the place to be. I remember at its peak, my dad said people were waitlisted up to two years. But now? Not so much."

He slips his phone back in his pocket, giving me a let's-get-down-to-business stare. "What are my options?"

*Um...your options would be...none, sir.*

I shake my head. "I don't really think there is anything you can do, other than clean it out and wait and see if the town comes back to life in the next few years?"

"What?"

"You could keep it as a vacation home?" I say. Preston popping in and out of town, just across the street from me. What could go wrong?

"I see." A gold watch that probably costs more than my car glints as it catches the sunlight when he moves his wrist to check the time. "So, I can't sell?"

"No. I'm sorry but I'm afraid there hasn't been any interest in months. There's two other families ahead of you waiting to sell."

And one of those buildings just happens to be a castle...

Like, a real one.

One no one wants.

"Damn." He runs his hand over the back of his neck in a way that makes me ache for him. He glances at the tree-lined street behind him. "I noticed this place looked even quieter than before. Which I didn't think was possible."

"Yeah, sorry." I feel bad for laying this on him—no matter how much he hates this town. I also am finding myself staring at him a little too hard. I look down at the tops of my white sneakers. They could use a wash.

He gives a sigh. "Well, I guess I'll clean it up and wait. Are you the town real estate agent or something?"

"Yes, the real estate agent, church social director, yoga instructor and once a week I'm a librarian. But those gigs don't really pay anything." I have a few other titles I don't mention to him:

live-in nurse, reality television marathon binge watcher, and...

*Virgin loser who lives with her dad.*

"And you live here? With the reverend?" He looks up at the house.

"Yeah," I say.

He gives a low whistle, shaking his head. "God, your dad hated me. Called me the Devil a few times if I remember correctly."

"In my father's defense?" I say, "You know, he's the town preacher and you were the king of whiskey and women the year you lived here."

"Yeah. Whiskey helped me make a lot of really bad decisions, and I don't regret a single one." He gets lost in reminiscing, his eyes going distant for a moment, but then he's back, those blue-green pools locking on mine and making my knees go weak. "Hey, did you ever tell anyone about—that night?"

"No. No way." A shiver runs down my spine just thinking about what almost happened. "My dad would have killed me if he knew about it."

"Yeah. He...would've been furious." A heavy silence falls between us for a moment.

A slow smile spreads across his face. "But the end of the night? Damn. That was pretty special. I may have bragged to a few friends. It's not every day you hook up with a cheerleader in her cherry red convertible."

"You didn't..." I'm dying inside thinking of his friends talking about our hot little make out session. *Jules. Get a grip. You were sixteen.*

"Speaking of that night." He's already moved on, craning his neck and searching the driveway behind me. "Where is that sexy little car of yours?"

"Err..."

His eyes land on my new-to-me fifteen-year-old Toyota Camry.

He nods toward the car. "Is that your old man's? Looks like a pastor's car if I ever saw one. Where's yours?"

Lie, Jules. Tell him your hot little ride is in the shop.

I blurt out the truth. "That *is* my car."

"Oh, nice," he quickly recovers. "Great gas mileage."

"Yeah. And enough cup holders for an army."

He glances around. "Not much has changed here, huh?"

"Nope. When I came back it was kind of like being delivered to my doorstep by a time machine."

"*You* really haven't changed." He stares at me in a way that makes me feel naked, bared to him. I know what he sees. Twenty-something, living at home, driving an ugly car, working for the church, and still a—

"Wait, you're not still a..." His brow narrows as he stares at me, the tip of his tongue sliding across his full lower lip.

"Ugh! Seriously, Preston?" I cut him off before the next word can roll off his tongue. "What is wrong with you? That's not something you ask someone! Especially when it's the first time you've seen them in ten years."

My face has to be as red as my hair. I can feel it.

He throws his hands up in that surrender gesture again. "Sorry. I'm a lawyer. Gotta give you the third degree."

I cross my arms over my chest and give him the look I reserve for my unruly Sunday school children. "No. You really don't."

He leans up against the trunk of my pecan tree like he's planning on staying awhile. "In a way, though, it kinda feels like no time has passed. Between us, I mean...right?"

That's a dangerous question.

Because right now I feel like I'm sixteen, back in my cheerleading uniform wanting him to kiss me. I can almost taste the whiskey on his lips from that one crazy night.

I shrug. "I plead the fifth."

He presses on. "So, you're waiting for the one, huh? Waiting for marriage?"

"I'm not. Not really." Why am I talking to him about this? My face feels hotter. "Preston...seriously..."

*Please. Shut. Up.*

How do you admit that the kids at home didn't want you because you were the pastor's kid, the men in the city found you pretentious and goody-goody, and then your father got sick and your glamorous life in the city got shut down before you could burn your V-card and now you're stuck binge-watching other people's lives in your childhood bedroom?

And yes, you are still very much a virgin. A twenty-five-year-old virgin.

Doesn't matter whether I tell him, does it?

He can read it on my face.

There's a giant freaking V on my forehead right next to the L for loser.

"I should go back in," I say. I've suffered enough humiliation for one afternoon.

"I've overstayed my welcome," he says.

He puts his hand on my shoulder. I find myself leaning into him. He brings his face closer to mine.

Is he going to kiss me?

He brushes his lips over my cheek. "Bye, Jules."

It's chaste, but I'll take it. My skin tingles where he kissed me. "K, bye."

Please get out of my driveway now so I can breathe again.

And eat away my humiliation with a dozen cookies.

Oh, and investigate the dead body in my wall.

His gaze wanders from my eyes down the length of my—toned because there isn't anything else to do here but work out—body. His gaze settles around the inch of bare midriff my tee shows off, leaving a trail of heat over my skin. "It's really good to see you, Jules."

"You too, Preston." So good that my thighs seem to be permanently pressed together.

He turns on his heel, gliding back to his gold Land Rover. He slides in the driver's seat, giving me a wave. He backs down my driveway.

I watch his car until it's out of sight.

My heart starts beating again, breath filling my lungs.

With the devil from my past gone, it's time to switch gears. I've got a possible dead body to dispose of and a missing might-be-an-axe-murderer father to find.

Right after I have one more cookie.

## 2

# Preston

My dad's place is just the same as I remember it, outdated with dark wood furniture and shag carpeting. The slight scent of cigar smoke hangs in the air. I'm sure if I open the cabinet above the fridge—yep. There it is. A half-empty bottle of whiskey.

Or half full depending on whether you're an optimist.

I pull myself a generous tumbler of the stuff. I'm an incredibly optimistic person. I sip it as I walk around my dad's sad house.

Dishes, clothes, a baseball card collection. There's so much shit to pack up. I pour another whiskey. I could have just paid someone to do the job for me but that felt pretty sacrilegious, sending someone else to do this job, even if my father and I weren't close.

Was this house the only reason I came back to this backward town? Or was there a vision of a pretty little redhead from my past beckoning me like a siren?

No, I tell myself. My motives were purely altruistic. I had no idea she would be here.

Last I'd heard she was living in the city. When I think of her, I picture her all dressed up in her couture knockoffs, smiling and flirting and dancing at bars, hundreds of men ogling her from the sidelines.

When a woman with red hair walks by me at a club, I take a second glance to make sure it isn't her.

It never is.

*Is* she still a virgin?

I think of the rosy blush that bloomed over her cheeks when I tried to ask her. She cut me right off. God, Preston, what an asshole move. You don't see her for ten years, then you ask her the status of her virginity?

I chuckle, sipping at my whiskey.

*Yeah*...she's most definitely a virgin.

I could be her first. My cock stirs and a warmth presses against the center of my chest. A possessive wave of heat overtakes me, making my balls ache and my bones feel restless.

Preston—get a grip. You're here all of, what? A week? Then you're back to your life and she's back to hers.

I open closets, looking at piles of junk. It's a lot of stuff. This *might* take weeks. A month, even. Especially if I keep consuming whiskey at this rate.

I'd better keep drinking.

If I couldn't get her out of my mind then, I certainly won't be able to now. Hell—she's right across the street. I left the law firm in good hands. I've got an eager intern wanting to learn the ropes sitting at my desk. He's probably doing a better job of it than me. I could hang around awhile. Get this place in order.

*See what happens...*

I change into jeans and a button-down flannel shirt, hoping I'm dressed appropriately for my outing. My friend Rich gave me a gift before I left. *When in the backcountry might as well play the part,* he said, handing me a pair of snakeskin boots with heels and pointed toes encased in silver.

I stare down at my feet. "Damn. These are ugly as hell." Rich's idea of a joke. I'd trade them for my tan leather Koio's, but I'm going to need them for what I'm about to do.

I've got to accomplish something tonight, other than destroying my liver. I need boxes to pack up my dad's stuff. And I've got a blind date.

When they built this town, they erected a stone wall around the whole thing, closing it with a drawbridge. Crazy, right? What's even crazier than having a massive wall wrapping around your property and your own private drawbridge? They enacted a curfew of 10 pm. The gates are locked after that.

One of many reasons I hated it here.

As I made my way into town, Beau was the guard at the drawbridge. He's the last standing Jones, the family that runs a cattle ranch in Cedar Creek, a blonde-haired blue-eyed boy next door type who couldn't bear to leave his childhood home behind. He's no longer operating a cattle ranch, but he kept the horses.

We got to talking. He's got empty boxes and a truck I can borrow, and he was telling me about one of his girls that I could spend some time with. I signed right up, not wanting to die of boredom on my first night.

My watch tells me I'd best get going.

My father's house is on the main road with all the other neatly manicured homes. I walk down the cobblestone sidewalk, waving to the curious stares I receive from the residents as I head down to the old Jones ranch.

A creek runs along the side of the road, babbling to me as it streams over river rocks. This place is quaint, even charming. It could almost be a little weekend getaway from the city. If they had a bar, a club, and an all-night breakfast place.

A split-rail fence lines the property. Beau's waiting for me by the gate in the fencing. "Hey, Preston. I didn't think you'd show." He gives me an open, friendly smile.

"Hell, I'm a sucker for a good deal. When you said lessons were buy-one-get-one, how could I say no?"

"You can take the man out of the city, but you can't take the city out of the man. When it came down to actually getting on the back of a horse for the first time, I thought you might back out."

"I'm always up for a little adventure," I say. "Besides, I love surfing. How different can this be?"

"Right." The impish grin on his face tells me it could be a lot different.

We walk up to a coppery red horse.

"Hey, girl." Beau pats her neck. "This is Cinnamon, the Appaloosa mare I was telling you about. She's a great ride. Gentle but fast."

I must be in need of a good lay because between him saying *she's a great ride* and the color of Cinnamon's reddish coat, I'm reminiscing about Jules in those tight jeans and cropped tee she was wearing today, the peek-a-boo inch of her midriff beckoning me.

"She's beautiful." I reach out and pat the horse's snout.

Cinnamon gives her mane a shake, throws her head back, and sneezes right in my face.

"What the—" I dab at my face with the back of my sleeve.

"Whoa, girl!" Beau hands me what I hope is a clean rag from his back pocket. "Sorry about that. Maybe she's allergic to your cologne?"

"Maybe," I say, mopping up my face. I've been on the ranch for two minutes and I'm already ready for a hot shower. "It's just some aftershave lotion."

A half hour later my ass is asleep, my boots are covered in mud, and Cinnamon has gone on strike, standing frozen in the center of a field. She's not impressed with me. I think it's these hideous boots.

I cut my lesson short and head home with the truck and boxes.

I take the world's longest shower in my dad's too-small, grimy, tiled tub. I haven't even been here twenty-four hours and I already miss my life at the Village, the endless hot water in the tankless heater, my massive rain shower, my heated floors, my heated towel bar...

And I'm craving a slab of Charlie Bachman's lasagna. She and the other Beauties keep bachelors like me fed; casseroles and pasta dishes fill our fridges. I want dinner from home. And an ice-cold microbrew from that place on Fifth Street.

I dry off and get dressed in jeans and a black tee—a casual kind of outfit I haven't worn in a long time. I go to my dad's fridge. It's empty with the exception of an opened box of baking soda and a quart of outdated milk. I hold my breath while I pour the curdled stuff down the sink. The freezer's no better. The only things in there are two expired microwave dinners. I toss them in the trash.

"What the hell did the man eat?" I think of my time here with him. Did we eat every meal in town? I think we did.

I guess that's where I'll go.

I ramble down the street only to find the café closed up for the night, its windows dark.

I have half a mind to find Jules' number and call her—she seems like a woman who can cook.

The porch light is on over her red front door. I'm staring at it, starving, and debating making a total ass of myself by knocking on her door and asking what's for dinner.

I hear a furious scream. And then thumping.

It's coming from her house and it sounds a hell of a lot like Jules is in trouble. I jog across the street, knocking on her front door like I did earlier that day. The yelling stops.

"Jules? Are you okay?" I bang my fist against the door. "Jules? Open up."

I'm about to break down her front door. I'm checking out the hinges, trying to figure out what tools I need to grab from my dad's garage or if I'm just going to try and kick it down when the door opens.

Jules peeks her head out. She's holding the door open a crack, like she's hiding something behind her. She looks fine. What the hell was all that screaming about?

Her brows rise in surprise when she sees it's me. "Preston? What are you doing here?" She peeks over her shoulder, a panicked look settling into her face.

"I heard yelling." I put my hand against the frame of the doorway. I'm not leaving until I find out what's going on.

She shakes her head. "It's nothing." But there's worry flashing in her blue eyes.

I pry. "Is it your dad? Did you guys have a fight?"

"No." She shakes her head. "I haven't exactly...found him yet."

"Found him? I thought he was out when I came by earlier?"

"Oh, yeah," she says. "I meant, he's not home yet."

Who else would she be yelling at? The idea of an abusive boyfriend pops up in my mind. I'll kill him. "Then who's here? Why were you shouting?"

She holds my gaze, staring at me but not speaking.

"Jules." I give her my best lawyer face, demanding an answer.

She cracks. "Everything is fine. I promise."

I stare harder.

She can tell I'm not buying it.

She heaves a sigh. "Look. I'll come out." She steps out on the stoop, quickly pulling the door shut behind her.

She crosses her arms over her chest like she's cold. I wish I had a jacket to offer her. She looks at me. "See? I'm fine."

"Tell me what the screaming was about."

She looks down at her sneakers, avoiding my eyes. "I was just…frustrated. I have some personal issues going on and I was just blowing off some steam."

"What kind of issues?" I ask.

"I'm not trying to be rude, I promise, but why do you care?" She finally brings her eyes up to mine and stares at me with those baby blues.

It's a legit question.

Why *do* I care? I think back to that night, the feel of the heat of her skin against mine, my hand slipping up her skirt, sliding her panties to the side…

I clear my throat, adjusting my pants. "I just do. Let me help you. What's going on?" I sink down onto her stoop, grabbing her hand and pulling her down beside me. Her hand feels soft and small in mine, and somehow like it belongs there. I hate to let it go.

She folds her knees up, wrapping her arms around them. "Where to start?" She gives a gruff chuckle.

I pop into lawyer mode. My voice drops, my brows set. "Start with the most pressing issue."

"Okay." She takes a deep breath. "My dad. He's got this illness. We don't really know what it is yet. We've been to a lot of doctors and the bills are starting to add up."

"So, money problems? Is that the root of your stress?"

She nods. "Yeah. That's a pressing issue."

There's more she's not telling me. A need to control rises in me. I want to demand she tell me the whole truth and nothing but the truth.

Her pretty hair falls in soft curls over her shoulders. I need to touch it. I reach out, tucking a strand of hair behind her ear. I leave my fingers in her hair. "I can help you."

"Can you?" She holds my eye, an inkling of trust easing into her gaze.

"Yes. But you have to do something for me first." I pull her closer, my mouth a beat away from hers.

"What?" Her pearly teeth sink into her full bottom lip.

My stomach rumbles. "Feed me. For the love of God. The café is closed and my dad has no food in his house. Please, I'm begging."

A pretty laugh bubbles up from her throat. "Okay. But you know, my house is a mess. We're, ah, having some renovations done, and—it's a beautiful night. I pack a mean picnic. Give me ten minutes?"

"I can help," I say. I'm getting the feeling that there's more going on in there than just renovations and I want to investigate.

She's already getting up, brushing invisible dirt from the seat of her jeans. "No. Really. I'm type A to the max. I'd die right here on this stoop if you saw my house in such a mess."

I'll get to the bottom of this. Maybe not tonight but before I leave. "Okay. I'll wait out here."

She slips in the house, closing the door behind her.

I sit alone, looking up at the stars. With so few lights out here, the sky is so clear you can see the Milky Way. I spend the time searching for the constellations I learned in an astronomy elective in college. I start with the Big Dipper, the Little Dipper then move on to Orion, Taurus, and Gemini. Next, I spot Aquarius, Aries, and Leo.

She's back in eight minutes, a woven old-fashioned picnic basket on her arm, a red and white checkered tablecloth tossed around her neck. She's freaking adorable. The kind of woman you want to raise your kids...

Preston. Get a grip.

I stand to greet her. "I'll carry that." I reach for the basket.

"I've got it."

I don't argue. I just take the basket from her. She goes to take it back, but I give her that devastatingly charming look the ladies like and it works, makes her swallow her words.

"How about one of those bistro tables?" I nod to the closed café.

"Actually?" She shoots me a shy look. "There's this really cool spot up by the castle. A pretty meadow that overlooks the town."

"Sounds perfect."

We hike up the hill, making small talk as we go. I ask her about her many jobs for the town.

"I run the library on Fridays. On Sundays, I organize the church picnic, though our numbers are dropping. We might move it to a monthly thing instead of weekly." I can tell the words pain her to say. "And then I teach yoga a few times a week. We don't really have a gym or anything so I got certified so I could share some fitness with the town. It's fun for the most part—oh, except when Ms. Ray somehow got twisted into a pretzel last week and I had to help her untangle herself."

"Sounds..." Awful? Hellish? "Fun?"

"It's not for everyone. I know that." She gets a look on her face caught somewhere between a grimace and a grin—clearly unimpressed with how little I like this place. "What have you been up to?"

"I'm a lawyer. For the family."

"Ah—the Bachmans," she says, unimpressed. "When I lived in the city I heard so many rumors about you guys and your secret club."

"Secret club?" I laugh. More like a deadly mafia. I take the cases that come in from outside the family. We sure as hell like to keep our secrets, and it's easier to do if we have the presence of a normal law firm to distract from our stickier cases. "I guess it's something like that."

Her nose crinkles adorably as she looks up at me. "Is it true that women can only join by marriage?"

"Yes. Why? Are you interested?" I tease.

"Me? No. *Not* my thing." She gives her head an emphatic shake. "Just curious."

Not her...thing?

What does that even mean? Women in the city are lined up trying to get a guy like me. Wait—that sounded cocky. Was that cocky? But seriously—with the way we treat our women, who wouldn't want to be a Bachman Beauty?

Jules, I guess.

I catch a glance at her makeup-free face. She is perfectly comfortable in who she is; she wears her skin like a queen wears a robe. Jules Verduce knows who she is and what she stands for. And she's a small-town girl interested in helping others. But what if she got a taste of our lives? We're a very philanthropic bunch...

Why do you care, Preston? The most you can stretch this trip is a few weeks, then you're out of this dump and leaving her behind.

*For the second time.*

What am I hoping to achieve while I'm here?

We reach the meadow she's scoped out. Damn. It's beautiful up here. I almost find myself liking this little town.

We're high enough you can look out over the nearby towns, lights sparkling across the dark expanse in little clumps. My gaze follows the road down from the castle to Main. Soft orange streetlights dot the street, glowing over the cobblestones. The moon is high and full, and it lights the night. Moonbeams glitter over the water as it trickles along in the creek.

I help her lay the cotton tablecloth over the grass. She sinks down, neatly folding her legs beneath her.

Yoga's paying off.

I plop down beside her with far less grace. My curiosity wins out over playing it cool. "Tell me. What part of being a Bachman woman wouldn't be your thing?"

She gives a cute little snort. "I'd never let a man tell me what to do. You know...no offense, but I've heard you all are kind of..."

"Controlling?" I ask.

"Exactly," she says.

"Have you ever been under the control of a man before, Jules? It can be pretty fun." I flash her a grin.

Her face goes red and her mouth flops open.

I lift the lid to the basket, letting her stew on that for a moment. "I'm starving. What did you whip up for us?"

"Oh, nothing too special," she mumbles, her face heated from my flirting.

There's nothing short of a feast in that basket. Cold grilled chicken strips, hummus and sliced bell pepper, wedges of cheese and an array of crackers are spread between us. She even made a fruit tray.

She pulls out a plate of chocolate chip cookies. "And for dessert? Cookies."

I'm starting with dessert. I grab a cookie from the plate. It's still warm. I take a bite and it melts in my mouth. "That's really good."

"I'm glad you like it."

We eat in a comfortable silence, looking out over the soft lights of the town. "I have to admit, it really is a beautiful little place."

"I know." She gives a sigh. "I just wish more people would realize it. I'm afraid Cedar Creek is dying. But that's the least of my problems..." Her words trail off.

The moonlight brightens her skin, giving her the glow of an angel. I suddenly want to make everything right for her, be her knight in shining armor, slay all her dragons.

After what we went through together...all those years ago...we share a bond.

However fragile.

I'm a solver. I hate to dwell on the problem at hand. I want a solution.

I dive right in. "I want to help. Let's talk. It sounds like you need money. I can help you with that."

"You mean, give me money?" Her nose crinkles. It'd be adorable if I didn't think it was crinkling in disdain toward me.

"Sure. I've got plenty. I'd love to share some with you."

She shakes her head, setting her half-eaten cookie down and brushes her hands off. "No. No way. I can't take your money. I wouldn't be able to live with myself."

The moonlight brightens her flawless skin. The blue-tinged glow reminds me of that night, so long ago, when fate intertwined our lives. Something in me shifted that night. And it wasn't just the ripples that passed through my life after the chaos.

*She* shifted something inside me.

Denial is a fickle mistress. You can tell yourself what you want to hear, but eventually, the truth will show itself to you. I can't keep pretending I'm the player, the bad boy. That I'm never going to settle for one girl.

I should be fighting my attraction, there should be a thousand doubts running through my head right now. But I can't fight my feelings. And I don't have a single doubt.

I want her.

I want her now, just like I wanted her then.

I could have sent a dozen staff to have my dad's house ready for market in a day. And yes, it's true I felt it should be me packing up my father's belongings, but there was another reason I got in my Land Rover and drove out here...

Her. On the sliver of a chance that she might be here.

I'm finally ready to admit the truth to myself...

I've never, ever stopped thinking about Jules.

I want to kiss her. I want to own her. I want to make her mine.

"I know you don't want to take my money." I reach out, running a finger down the curve of her cheek. "What if you gave me something in exchange? Something you need, for something I want."

She moves in closer, melting into my touch. Her blue eyes search mine. "Look around, Preston. What could I possibly have to give you?"

My fingertips brush over the soft fullness of her lower lip. "Give me what I want and when I'm gone, you never have to see me again.

You'll have more money in your bank account than you know what to do with."

"And what do you want?"

Cupping her chin in my hand, I watch her face as I deliver my simple, one word answer.

"You."

## 3

# Jules

He can't be serious. But he is. He's staring at me, gauging my reaction.

I'm speechless.

"Give me you," he says.

"You want to buy my... virginity?"

"I do. You said you weren't waiting for anything special. But I want more than just that. I want you, all of you, while I'm staying here."

All of me? What does that even mean? And how did we get here?

Why did I let out that scream? Finally brave enough, I'd decided to haul my dead body to the kitchen so I could cut into the plastic and at least peek inside. The darn thing was so heavy I couldn't even get it out of the closet.

The weight of my life all came crashing down on my shoulders. The mystery illness with my dad, the mounting debt, seeing Preston after all these years looking so handsome and happy and successful, while knowing that my life has slowed to a stop. I *may* have screamed in frustration.

Causing my knight in golden armor to come running...

"What do you think, Jules?" he asks.

"What do I think..." My words trail off. Why do my panties suddenly feel damp? I inch back from him. "What do you mean, give you *all of me?*"

"You," the tip of his tongue drags across his bottom lip, "submit to me. Give me your submission. Let me lead you, in and out of the bedroom."

Holy hotness.

Talk about an indecent proposal.

Submission. A strange, sexy word that's so not in my vocabulary. Why is the thought of submitting to him making this self-proclaimed feminist feel like a horny teenager? Now I'm not only wet, my core is humming, my sex clenching. I press my thighs together, a feeble attempt to calm my aching desire.

I've read the books. I've seen the movies. I know what it means to submit yourself sexually, but reading and watching it are one thing. Sure, I've fantasized about a man taking charge of me in the bedroom—heck, all I've done is fantasize about men when it comes to the bedroom—but living it in your imagination and actually doing it are two very different things.

With the help of a glass of wine I might be able to pull off the bedroom side of things but outside the bedroom? I'm not a submissive woman.

But he's so...hot. And I'm so...curious. And my body is humming his name.

"How much money are we talking about?" I can't believe those words just came out of my mouth. Am I seriously considering his proposition?

The good girl preacher's daughter selling her virginity to the bad boy billionaire?

He can see I'm contemplating it. He takes the opportunity to lean over and whisper a number in my ear. A very big number. With a lot of zeros.

It's enough money to change my father's life. To make sure his bills are not only paid but with some careful investing, he'd be able to retire. Using my body to pay for it, though? If my father ever found out, I wouldn't need the money because the reverend would keel over and die.

I eye Preston.

He wouldn't tell anyone. No one but the two of us would have to know. Would they? I trust Preston. We've both kept our secret from that night; why couldn't we keep this one?

Still. This is a huge decision. "I need the night to think about it."

He does that whole *hands in the air trying to look innocent* thing, his brows flying up. "Of course! You should take the night. It's a big decision."

"Yes, it is."

"Because if you say yes, you're all mine." And he smiles that smile of his. The one that makes me want to say yes to all the bad decisions.

Heat flashes through my breasts, my nipples tightening and straining uncomfortably against the lace of my bra. What does he plan on doing with me? The throbbing between my thighs gets worse.

I can barely breathe.

I go to stand. "I need to get going."

"Let me help you pack up."

There's a palpable sexual tension running between us as we put lids on dishes. My arm accidentally brushes against his as we pack away the food and a thousand tiny electric pulses dance over my skin.

Having him this close to me with his indecent proposal hanging in the air between us, it's unnerving.

I can't think straight around him.

I need to be alone.

He walks me to the house. "You going to invite me in?" He says it teasingly, already knowing what my answer will be.

"Sorry. Not tonight."

There's that strained moment between two people that comes after a date—wait, was this a date?—where I'm wondering if he's going to kiss me, and he's wondering if he should try.

Preston goes for what he wants. He scoops his hand around the back of my head, bringing me close. "Good night, Jules," he murmurs into my lips, the vibrations of his words tickling my skin.

And he's kissing me. Heat and desire and magic dance through my body and I'm right back there, in the cherry red convertible, his tongue slipping into my mouth. I need to stop this kiss. It feels too good and I'm afraid I'll lie down right here on this stoop and beg him to take my virginity.

I press a polite hand against his chest.

He pulls away. "See you tomorrow?"

"Sure."

He waits to make sure I get in okay. I slip inside a tiny crack in the door, just in case my dead body's up and moved while I've been gone. Closing the door, I lock it and slump to the floor, my back pressed into the wood, my head in my hands.

My skin is hot and I'm sure I'm as red as a tomato right now. "Jules Verduce. What have you gotten yourself into?"

I have the night. I decide to shove the whole "am I going to sell myself" debate away for later. I really need to find my dad and figure out what exactly is in my hallway.

No messages on my cell. I go to the landline. There's a red light blinking on our dinosaur of an answering machine. I push the button.

The woman's chipper recorded voice comes over the speaker.

*You have one new message! Thursday at nine twenty-three pm.*

I look at the clock. It's nine thirty. I just missed him. "Thanks," I tell her. "Please let it be Dad."

*Hey hon, it's Dad.*

Thank goodness.

*I'm in Rosebery tonight. It totally slipped my mind to tell you but I have a specialist appointment really early in the morning, so I got a hotel—didn't want to be late. They're going to be doing some testing, so I'll be here for three nights total. I'm staying at the Village Inn right off the highway. I hope that's okay. It's the cheapest rate I could find. I'll be back early on Saturday.*

My heart pings. I wish he could stay in a nice hotel and not have to worry about the cost.

Preston's indecent proposal pops up in my mind. With that kind of money my dad could stay at the Taj Mahal, and we'd still be okay. I shove down the thought of the easy money, reminding myself of the price tag it comes with.

Dad leaves the number for the front desk. He still hasn't gotten on board with the cell phone craze. He's been a little spacey lately. It's too late to call his room, he's probably sleeping after the drive, but I want to at least confirm he's really there. I dial the front desk.

"Hi there. I think my dad's staying there for the next few nights. Could I get his room number and confirm the dates?" Everything checks out. Dad's safe and he's getting the testing he needs.

This deserves a cup of cocoa. Making my way to the kitchen, I take a deep breath. The body's lying half in and half out of the closet where I left it when I gave up and screamed. I nudge at it with the toe of my sneaker.

Still dead.

I'll have to call Dad tomorrow for an explanation.

Tonight? I just don't want to look at it anymore. Out of sight, out of mind.

"Heave, ho!" I push and pull and prod until it's all the way inside the closet and I can shut the door. I sweep up the drywall dust that's escaped into the hall and wipe the hardwoods with a damp cloth.

I stand back, taking in my handiwork. Someone could come into the house now and have no idea my father's started a closet mortuary.

Perfect.

Time for pj's, cocoa, and a happy little rom-com.

There's a knock at the door as I'm taking my first sip. Not the three clean raps that signal it's Preston, but five hard bangs.

"Who on earth could it be?" I look at my watch. It's 10:15. Most of the town is snoring by now.

I'm expecting Ms. Clancy needing me to come next door and help her find her glasses. Instead, there's a tall man with dark wavy hair, deep brown eyes and the widest set of shoulders I've ever seen. He speaks with a bit of a British accent as he says, "Miss Jules?"

"Ah—yes?" My voice squeaks with surprise. "I'm...she?"

"Hello, love. Richmond Bachman. Pleasure to make your acquaintance. I have a delivery for you from Mr. Preston Bachman."

I peek around him at my driveway. There's a sleek black sedan parked behind my Camry. "How did you get past the drawbridge?"

He shrugs. "I'm a Bachman."

"Okay." So these men are as powerful as they say. "Um…is that for me?" I nod to the stack of satiny, silver packages in his hands. There are three in a tier, and the whole thing is all wrapped up with a sexy black bow.

"Yes. Special delivery." He hands me the boxes. "For the lady of the house."

I take them. They're surprisingly light. The material feels cool and slippery against my skin. "Thank you."

"My pleasure." He gives me a nod.

He's such a tough, rugged-looking man, the big muscles, the olive skin, the dark hair and eyes, that the accent is throwing me off.

"Um, do you need help getting out? I could call Beau?"

He nods in the direction of the entrance to town. "He's waiting for me at the bridge. Nice bloke."

"Well, thanks for coming all this way and bringing me"—I glance down at the mystery boxes—"this."

"You have a good evening, Miss Jules." He smiles with rows of straight, white teeth.

"You too, Richmond."

I wait till I see him open his car door, then I go to close mine, but his deep voice stops me as he calls out, "And Jules?"

"Yes?"

He flashes me another smile, showing me his one dimple on his left cheek. "Preston. He's a good man. One of the best."

"Um...okay? Thank you?" I offer a smile and a wave.

He climbs into his car, revving the powerful engine.

I close the door behind me, locking it.

Thank goodness my dad is not here.

Lucky for me, he is out of town. There've been more men at my doorstep in the last few hours than in the past two years. The reverend could not handle it.

There's a card on top in a crisp white envelope, my name swooping across the front in black ink.

I take the boxes to our dining table. It's just a folding card table set up in the kitchen, but I've dolled it up, covering it with a floral cloth and a vase of fresh flowers I picked from the backyard. I set the boxes on the table and they look so pretty all stacked up by size, I almost want to take a picture of them before I open them.

I haven't been given a gift in, well... years.

I sit down in a chair, pulling the card from the top of the box. I always open the card first and if I ever have kids, I'll teach them to do the same. I slip my fingernail under the edge of the back of the envelope and open it.

It's made of heavy, creamy paper. I love the feel of the stationary between my fingers. Preston took care with this.

*Jules,*

*I know I said I'd give you the night and I will.*

*I just felt you should have all the facts before you make your decision.*

*Preston*

"You can take the lawyer out of the courtroom, but you can't take the courtroom out of the lawyer." I laugh to myself, shaking my head.

I slip the card back in the envelope and set it on the table. I suddenly feel like a kid on Christmas morning. Which box to open first?

I start at the top, reaching for the smallest box.

Removing the lid reveals a neatly folded layer of tissue, little silver sparkles threaded through the delicate paper. Underneath is a phone. It looks a lot like the fancy one with all the buttons Preston's had.

I pull it from the box. The screen automatically turns on. There's a picture of a handsome cartoon devil on the screen, his muscles bulging, his white teeth flashing. "Nice, Preston."

Text pops up on the screen.

*New voice audio for Jules*

Instinctively, I reach out and tap the words. A recording plays. It's Preston's deep voice.

*Hey, Jules. I thought you might want to have another phone to communicate with me. One you can hide from your old man. It's a Bachman phone so you'll never lose reception, even in this Podunk town. And full disclosure? It has a tracker on it that reports to my phone. Let me know if you want it taken off, but I figured someone ought to be looking out for you.*

Aww...that's kinda sweet. Stalkerish, yes. But sweet.

Will he be able to tell where I am at all times? I make a mental note not to take this thing in the bathroom.

I know I should be freaked out by the amount of control over my life he's assumed he can have, but something deep down inside me likes that someone will actually know where I am. I've been caring for others for so long, it's kind of nice that someone is worrying about me for a change.

Is that selfish?

I don't mean to be selfish. Besides, I haven't made my decision yet. All these boxes could very well be repacked and returned to his doorstep tomorrow morning. I give myself a definitive nod of agreement. I'll open them—who wouldn't—but I won't let the gifts sway my decision.

Time for the second box.

I pull off the lid, peeling back the paper. Oh boy—it's a doozy. My face goes hot.

Laying in the box is a set of fancy underwear. Well, underwear is a stretch—I think there's more material in my facecloth than there is in this entire box. I pull a pair of silky black thigh highs from the box, careful not to snag them.

There's a thin black line running up the back of the stockings, rising up to meet a lacy band that wraps around your thighs. A black silk garter belt with snaps and a little bow on the front is next.

Then there's a scrap of a black satin thong. I lift it from the package only to find my face burning hotter as the material parts.

There's no crotch in these panties.

*Noooo* crotch. None. At. All.

The bra is nothing but two tiny triangles of see-through lace. Not nearly enough support for my girls. I check the tags. The brand looks to be French and the sizes are European but they all look like they will fit me.

Not that they'll be hiding much.

What could possibly be in the last box?

I'm almost scared to open it.

"Last one, Jules. You've got this." I pull the lid off and remove the tissue. Lying in the box is the most gorgeous shade of green I've ever seen. I reach out, fingering the silky fabric. It's so soft, such fine quality, I feel my breath catch in my chest.

Standing, I lift the garment from the box. It's a calf-length gown with a plunging neckline and a tie at the waist. My fashion blog was all about how to fake an expensive-looking wardrobe on a tight budget.

I sneak a peek at the label. *No way.* It's a Versace.

Never in my life have I owned a piece of couture. "It's gorgeous." I hug it against my body, being sure not to wrinkle it.

Suddenly I want nothing more than to wear this dress and all the sexy trappings that go under it.

But there's a catch.

It comes at a hefty price.

I'm keeping it either way. Preston will just have to understand. Or I'll beg him. I lift the last note from the bottom of the box.

*Jules,*

*If your answer is yes, then be waiting for me on your doorstep wearing my gifts, at eight o'clock tomorrow night.*

*Say yes.*

*Preston*

I tap my finger against the card. "Okay, Jules. You've had enough time. Make up your mind."

But I'm not a fly by the seat of my crotchless panties kinda girl.

I need a pros and cons list.

I pull out my notebook and a reliable pen.

I sit at the kitchen table, drawing a line down the center of the paper. I write PROS at the top of the left column and CONS at the top of the right.

"Hmm." I nibble at the end of the pen, the one bad habit I allow myself. "Pros. Pay off my dad's bills. Create a retirement account for him. Plan for my own financial future. Maybe have a little left over to help the town start some social clubs."

Okay, that's the pragmatic stuff taken care of. But let's be honest—there are more possible pros. I jot a few more down.

*I'm curious.*

*I'd lose my virginity before hitting twenty-six.*

*Preston is hot as hell.*

*This experience could be really sexy and really fun.*

*Getting to wear the dress somewhere other than my living room.*

"Now the cons." I nibble at the pen. "Hmm...other than possible eternal damnation and gut-wrenching parental disapproval, I really can't think of any."

But hey—I believe our God is a loving, forgiving God and my dad can't really judge my actions right now.

He's got a body in the closet, for heaven's sake.

The Bachman phone talks to me in a singsongy tone.

*Jules, you have a new message*

"I like you better than the answering machine." I pick up the phone, pressing the screen. It's a text from Preston.

*I can't wait any longer*

*What's it going to be*

My head feels light and my knees weak. I think I need to lie down. I go to my room and flop down on my bed, holding the phone to my face.

*Well, Jules,* I ask myself, *what's it going to be?*

My decision finally comes to me. If I'm going to do this, I'm going to do it on my terms.

Holding my breath, I text back my answer and hit *send*.

Dropping the phone on the comforter, I bury my face in my hands.

I just sold my soul to the Devil.

## 4

**P**reston

It's weird, sitting here in my dad's armchair, the cushions worn into the shape of his body. I take a long swig of my beer, wondering when it was we got so distant. When I was little, we'd play ball. He'd spend endless hours helping me work on my pitching.

He never missed one of my Little League games.

Then my parents split, my mom running off with one of her many younger boyfriends, taking me with her. When I was sixteen, my mom took off with her longest-standing boyfriend, Edwardo, doing a yearlong tour of Europe; I stayed with my dad. Got into a little trouble right before our year was up and didn't hear from my old man too much after that.

If it was me?

I'd never let my kid out of my sight. Not for a damn second. No matter what his mother wanted, or what he did. Family is family. It's part of why I joined the Bachman Family. We believe family first, family forever.

A nagging tension has been caught somewhere between my gut and my chest. At first, I thought it was heartburn. Upon deeper reflection and catching myself staring at a baby or two, I've realized it's the longing of wanting to settle down and start a family. I haven't brought it up with the guys. They wouldn't believe me.

They think I'm a serial playboy, that I'll never settle down. I guess I just haven't met the one…

Or maybe it's just that I haven't convinced a certain sweet little redhead that she's the one. Speak of the angel—is that my phone going off? I grab it from the side table.

It's her.

Jules:

*You get one date*

*We can do some…stuff*

*But no S$X*

"Come on, baby. You can spell the word out," I laugh. God, she's so sweet. It makes my cock want to explode.

I take another sip of the ice-cold beer to cool off.

There's more.

Jules:

*Here's my price*

And she's texted a measly number that wouldn't even cover my tab at Gotcha's Nightclub last weekend.

No deal.

I want her. All of her.

My fingers fly over the screen as I type my reply.

Jules

I'm not a nail biter, but right now I'm coming dangerously close. Nerves cartwheel through my belly as I wait for his reply.

I couldn't do it. I couldn't give him the all of me that he wanted. But I'll give him a little piece. I can't believe I'm even texting with him right now. He comes back into town all of a few hours ago and now we're negotiating the terms of a date?

This is impulsive. I don't do impulsive. My mom was always a free spirit, always ready to stop whatever we were doing to go off on the next adventure, or break plans if she had a wild hair to do something else.

I'm like my dad. A planner. I usually play it safe, but I'm enjoying this. It's exciting and fun and not at all what I expected for my evening.

Pins and needles dance over my skin while I wait for his reply. It feels like ages have gone by but my sexy new Bachman phone says it's only been twenty seconds since I sent my message.

Finally, his text comes.

Preston:

*That wasn't our deal, baby*

Oh, I know it wasn't, mister. I hate to tell you, but you can't just buy someone's virginity. It's a gift that has to be given to you. You can have a date…one date…maybe I'll toss in a few kisses and some…other stuff.

Besides, I think the price I've set is perfectly reasonable for an evening of my time.

And don't call me baby.

I type out my reply...

Preston

I stare at the screen of my phone. She's a feisty one, that Jules. I can't believe her response when I read it.

My sassy girl tells me it's off.

Jules:

*Then there is no deal #notyourbaby*

I'll get what I want. I shoot back a text.

Me:

*I think you should reconsider*

She doesn't respond.

Why the hell isn't she responding?

Me:

*I have quite a night planned*

*You're going to love it*

*You don't want to miss out*

*Say yes*

I've never had to wait this long for a woman I'm interested in to text me back. I'm not being a cocky ass—it's just the truth. Damn, this is infuriating. Heat flashes over my face and my skin starts to crawl. I hate this feeling.

Wait...

Is this how girls feel when you say you're going to call...

And they're sitting at home, staring at their phones....

Waiting for you to call...and you don't call them?

Damn. It sucks.

Guilty as charged.

I make a mental note to call them in the future. Or maybe just don't even tell them I'm going to call in the first place.

Can't tear my eyes from this stupid screen.

Why does Jules have such a dick hold on me?

Finally, her texts pop up.


Jules

My best night in the past two years was when I snuck a bottle of prosecco into my dad's house the night they finally released the first season of *Desperate Housewives of Vegas*. Can I really turn down his offer? If not for the money, just to have some fun? That's one thing Preston was known for when he lived here...

A good time.

For once in my life, I'm going to ask myself what I want. Do I want to go on this date? I dig a little deeper into my soul. Hottie from my past, man with lots of money who loves to spend it, most likely a killer night in the city. Should I make a pros and cons list? My little notebook beckons to me from the kitchen counter.

Live a little, Jules. You don't have to scratch out a list every time you need to make a decision. You know you want to go.

But he is *not* getting the seggs. I've seen girls use that word for the other one when they talk about spicy books on *BookTok*. I think it's cute. Maybe I should have sent him that instead of the S$X text...

Time to grow up, Jules. You can type out S-E-X to him. You won't die of humiliation.

My fingers hover over the screen. Okay, what am I going to write? I need to be clear. I need to set boundaries. He has to accept my terms.

Me:

*Sounds good*

*Pick me up at 8*

*One date*

*No S$X!*

I smile as my demands flow through the air across the street to his house.

Preston

Damn. She's a stubborn one. Fine. I'll let her think she's in charge.

Just this once.

Besides, there's so many things I can do to her that don't technically fall under the umbrella of *S$X*.

Me:

*Fine*

*One date*

*But I want the other stuff you mentioned earlier*

*And, baby?*

She waits a moment before responding. I can picture her pearly white teeth sunk into her bottom lip as she deliberates. Finally, two more texts come through.

Jules: *Yes? #notyourbaby*

Me: *You'd best triple your price*

I find my breath catching in my chest as I stare down at the screen, waiting.

Finally, one word comes through.

Jules:

*Deal*

*No S$X*

She makes me laugh out loud as I respond.

Me:

*Fine*

*But only if you can say the word out loud*

*Record it on your phone and send it to me*

I can practically see her blushing.


Jules

*He wants me to...what?*

Gah—why does he need me to do that? It's a control thing, isn't it? If there's one thing I know about Preston and Bachman men in general, they like to be in control.

More like, demand to be in control.

Now that I've committed, I really want this date.

He's humbly conceded. Kind of. He's agreed to my terms. The least I could do is whisper the word *sex* into the phone, right?

Deep breaths pull through my lungs like I'm prepping to sprint in the Olympics. I can do this. I just need a little something to help me. I go to find my gifts.

47

I stroke the Versace dress like she's a kitten. I want to wear her so badly.

I hit record.

Preston

It takes a full two minutes but finally I get an alert. *You have one voice text.* I press play and Jules' sweet little voice whispers out the word 'sex' so fast I almost miss it. And it sounds kind of like she's put *g's* on the end of it.

I play it again.

Did she say sex, or...*eggs?*

Maybe a combo? Seggs? Doesn't matter.

She obeyed to the best of her ability.

Cute.

Let's get her to do one more thing for me.

Me: *Baby?*

Jules: *Yes? #NOTYOURBABY*

I'm enjoying every second of this. I type, *Can you be a good girl and do one more little thing for me?*

Nothing...then...

Jules: *What is it?*

I chuckle as I type out my demands.

She's definitely blushing this time.

Jules

*Put on those pretty little lacy things I sent you and send me a picture*

I stare down at the bits of lace and string. Oh, heck no! And visual evidence? No way.

I shoot him a text.

Me: *NOT happening*

Preston: *Check your Venmo...and turn your notifications on for the app*

I do as he says, turning on the notifications for my Venmo so I'll be notified of deposits and then check the balance.

Holy cow.

He's dropped a few bars of gold in there.

He really wants this pic.

I'll give it to him.


Preston

Five full minutes go by before she replies.

Jules: *Give me ten minutes*

"Oh hell yes!" I shift my weight in my seat, my jeans growing uncomfortably tight in anticipation. I finish the beer while I wait.

*You've received a picture text.*

It's Jules. But it's not the photo my dick is aching for. The naughty little minx is wearing the bra as a mask, her blue eyes barely visible from behind the thin black lace triangles.

And the crotchless panties?

She's wearing them as a headband.

She's got a sassy little smile on her pretty face, thinking she's gotten away with something.

Me: *Cute*

*But put them on right or I'm coming over there*

Jules: *To do what?*

Ah, kitten wants to play?

Me: *To lay you over my lap and spank you for disobeying me*

No response. I give a chuckle.

Me:

*I know you read that text*

*And your face got all hot*

*And you got all wet between your pretty thighs*

*Thinking of what it would feel like to have me spank you*

*Didn't you, baby?*

*Do you want to slip your fingers in your panties*

*And see how wet you are for me?*

I throw another couple grand in her account and wait.

I know she got the notice that the money arrived.


Jules

I tear the bra-mask off my face and the panty-headband from my head. He's sent more money. And he's called me out.

Oh Lord, has the man called me out.

My panties are melting off of me, just from reading those seggsy—sexy—texts. He wants me to touch myself. To reach down between my thighs and see how wet he's making me. But I can't. Not for any amount of money.

I could never do that. I'm a good girl. A nice girl. I bake cookies for the elderly, lead choir for services on Sunday, and I've only just bought my first vibrator this year. Sure, I've explored—let's be honest, a few times a week, who hasn't—but I could never tell him that.

Me: *I...can't*

Him: *Why not?*

Me: *I don't do that kind of thing*

Him: *You don't touch yourself?*

Me: *Not really*

Him:

*You're lying to me.*

*Everyone touches themselves*

*Tell me*

*Did you ever lie in bed and stroke your pretty pussy*

*Thinking of me*

*And my fingers*

*Touching you under your little cheer skirt?*

It's too much. I turn off the phone. He told me I could have the night and I'm going to take it.

I change into my comfiest pajamas and snuggle down in my bed. I put both phones on my nightstand. My real one is on in case my dad needs me. Preston's is off so that he doesn't burn me to ashes with his fiery texts.

I need a good night of sleep after the day I've had. God—how much has happened in the eight hours since Preston blew back into town? First, my dad went missing. Then, the body. Then Preston shows up and brings all the feels back to the surface.

Not to mention his indecent proposal and the giant money drops he deposited into my account.

All those things shook me. But gosh, the texts. I think they hit me the hardest. Especially the last one.

*Tell me*

*Did you ever lie in bed and stroke your pretty pussy*

*Thinking of me*

*And my fingers*

*Touching you under your little cheer skirt?*

Yes, Preston. I did. And I think of you every single *effing* time I touch myself. Is that what you want to hear? That your desperate virgin can think only of you when her hands are between her legs?

*Fuck.*

There, I said it. I said the f word and I'm going to say it again.

*Fuckity, fuck, fuck, fuck.*

I roll around in bed, too restless to sleep. Finally, I grab a melatonin gummy from my nightstand. They always knock me out.

In the morning I wake, stretching and smiling under the sunlight pouring in my windows. Then I remember my dad's little project and Preston's proposal and my body fills with tension.

The texts he sent remain in the forefront of my mind. I pick at my breakfast. I skim over the news on my phone. My day is filled with typical Friday things. Helping at the school, chaperoning a field trip to a museum in a nearby town, then dinner alone.

I look at the clock. It's six. Two hours till our date. Finally, I turn on Preston's phone.

There are a few texts from last night.

*You still there?*

*Don't ignore me, baby*

*I know you're thinking of me*

And a pic. But the smarty-pants phone is asking for my fingerprint to view it. How the heck did he get my fingerprint installed into this thing? Geez, the Bachmans are something—

*Whoa.*

*Oh. My. Gawd.*

Heat burns my face and embers dance in my belly.

It's my very first...

What do they call them?

*Dick pic.*

He's totally naked, lounging on a bed of white sheets. He's looking right at the camera, his full sexy lips curved into a smile that can only be described as devilish.

The tanned skin of his bare, muscled chest goes on for miles, dipping into carved hip bones that point directly to...

*It.*

His...dick.

He holds it in his hands, stroking it. It's tall and proud and oh-so-massive.

Slick heat pools between my thighs.

He knew how I'd react, how shocked I'd be, how turned on he would make me.

You know what? I'm going to make him think of *me*. I'm going to pay him back and send him the sexiest damn picture he's ever seen. I'm going to make him stroke his big fat...cock...see, I can say cock and think of me for once.

I text him back

*Nice pic*

*I'm sending you that pic you wanted*

*I'm putting on my present right now*

I tear off my clothes, tossing my gray washed-out sports bra and granny panties into the trash can. That Jules is gone. For now. I slip into the bra, surprised by how supportive the sheer fabric is. Damn, the girls look sexy as hell. Now for the stringy thing.

The first time I try it on, I get my big toe caught in the lacy split of the crotchless panty, but somehow, I manage.

Holy hell. My curves are just as full and jiggly as always but being encased in the lace and string makes them look like they were meant to be full and jiggly.

I love it.

I love the way I look. I love the way I feel. A sense of sensual power rises in me. I grab that phone, push the little camera button, and point it right at my almost naked body and—

Before I can snap the picture, the camera shuts down, allowing for a text from him to take over the screen.

*Hell yes, baby*

*I'm coming over*

*Our date starts now*

*Be ready*

## 5

# Preston

I don't even knock. I open the door, letting myself in. "Jules?"

She comes around the corner.

*Fuuuuuuuuuuuuck.*

She's wearing the bra and panties I sent her.

And nothing else.

A groan rises deep from my core. "Good girl."

The black lace triangles can barely contain the full curves of her breasts. Her nipples are peaked, the outline of their outline just visible under the fabric.

And the panties.

My God, the panties.

The narrow triangle just covers her sex, the strings rise high on her hips.

Her cheeks are flushed, her eyes shining with excitement and nerves. She bites her bottom lip, her eyes grazing my face. "You like?"

"I love. Let me see the back."

She's shy, turning slowly, but she complies.

I lose my breath, heat rushing up from my cock through my chest. The curves of her ass are just perfect, the thin black lines of the G-string crisscrossing over her skin.

"Are you sure it's not...I don't know... too much?"

"Too much?" I make a slow circle around her, a panther eyeing his prey. "How so?"

"I don't know." She gives a little shrug, wanting to hide her beautiful body from my prying eyes. "It's not too...." Her last word she whispers likes there's someone else in the room who could hear her. "Slutty?"

"Well, if it's slutty..." I move to her. I run the pad of my thumb over her bare collarbone, sending shivers through her that make her shudder. I keep the trail going, my thumb moving down over the curve of her breast. I reach her nipple, patting a circle over the tight, hard little bud till she gasps. "Then you're my pretty little slut. Aren't you, baby?"

Her bottom jaw drops. Her face goes from pink to red. "You can't say stuff like that."

"Can't I?" I take her nipple between my thumb and forefinger and pinch. Her eyelids grow heavy and she gives a little shuddering sigh. "I can if you like it."

I leave her breast, walking my fingertips down her trembling belly. Her hands lay at her sides, her fingers opening and closing like they don't know if they want to pull me closer or push me away.

"Tell me. Do you like it? Do you want to be my pretty little slut?"

She presses her lips together.

Lightly, I run my fingers over the seam of her sex, my fingertips curled, beckoning her to answer me. I move closer to her, pressing my chest against the swell of her breasts as I touch her. My mouth is by her ear, my free hand sliding up the back of her neck, tangling in her hair.

"Tell me, baby," I whisper, my words hot against her skin. "Can I slide my fingers between your legs and see how wet you are for me? I want to see if you like being my pretty little slut. I want to see if those dirty words turn you on."

I kiss my way from her earlobe across her flushed cheek. My lips hover over hers. "Say yes, baby. Say yes."

My fingers stop moving and I wait.

Finally, she gives me the gift of one whispered word. "Yes."

I slip my fingers down, finding my way between the lacy folds of the crotchless panties. "Oh my God," I moan as my fingers glide over the heat of her slickness. "It feels so good to touch you again after all these years."

I was just teasing her when I said I bragged about our hook up. Just wanted to see her blush. I never told anyone about what we did in the back seat of her car.

I respect her too much to do that.

And I would have had to kick someone's ass if they made even one lewd comment about her.

But damn, I never forgot the feel of this magical pussy.

She gives a little whimper as she parts her thighs, giving me better access to stroke her.

I put my mouth on hers, kissing her like we did that night. The intensity and the boundless energy of that night comes back. I thrust my tongue into her mouth, exploring and tasting her as I press my finger inside of her sweet sex.

As I touch her, she kisses me back with ferocity. The good girls are always the naughtiest behind closed doors, aren't they? Her body is so responsive to my touch, melting against me, her kiss begging me for more.

I add a second finger to the first. She's so tight a little whine rises from her as she stretches to accommodate me. I break our kiss just long enough to pull my fingers from her and show them to her.

They glisten with her arousal. "See how wet you are for me?" I hold her gaze as I slip them in my mouth and taste them.

She gives a little gasp, turning away from me in shame.

I capture her chin, bringing her back to me. I kiss her, letting her taste her own sex. My fingers go back to her panties, gathering more slickness. I find her clit, making slow circles around the little bud.

Her hands find my shoulders. She moans into my mouth. Her hips start to sway, moving against me in time with my fingers. My pretty little dancer. I stroke her and she sings little whimpers in her kisses.

I break our kiss but keep teasing her with the fingers of one hand and with my other, I grab her ass. "You're a good girl wearing what I told you, but you were naughty last night, weren't you, baby? That cute little trick you pulled with your mask and your headband. You really ought to be spanked for that, shouldn't you?"

My words make her hips grind against me. I go back to kissing her, pull my palm away and give her ass a nice, stinging spank.

"Mmm..." She loves it. Her fingers dig into me as she rises up on the tiptoes of her bare feet. Her body presses harder against mine. She's greedy for more. Her hips buck against me. I spank her again, my hand landing on the fullness of her curves. I love the way her flesh jiggles under my palm.

I move my fingers faster, spanking her ass again.

She breaks away from my mouth. "Oh my gosh. Oh my. Make me come."

Pretty little words straight from the preacher's daughter's mouth.

"If I can make you feel this good with just my fingers, imagine what I can do with my—"

We're interrupted by someone banging on the door.

*No. Fucking. Way.*

Her eyes fly open, dragging toward the door. "Oh shoot!"

"Jules! Jules, are you home?" the voice rings out.

She pushes me away. "Oh shoot! I totally forgot!"

"It's okay. You can say it. Fuck. Say it for me, pretty baby." She's adorable. "What did you forget?"

"Stop," she hisses as she pulls away. "He's at the *door.*"

"Who?"

"Doesn't matter." Her face is red and she pulls away from me. "I've got to change!"

I grab her arm, pulling her back.

"What *are* you wearing?" I pull her closer. I look her over, committing every detail of her body in that lingerie to memory. "Do you always dress like this for company?"

*"Preeeeessssston,"* she pleads. "Let me go."

The knocking returns. "Jules! You home? I see your lights on."

Who is this man knocking at my girl's door? It's time for me to meet him.

I let her go. "You go throw on something decent. I'll get the door."

She scurries off to her room and I watch her cheeks jiggle as she leaves. "And Jules?"

She stops, glancing over her shoulder at me. "Yes?"

"You really shouldn't wear such scandalous clothes. Someone might try to steal your virginity."

"You are infuriating, Preston Bachman," she groans, tossing me a look a teacher would give a naughty schoolboy.

Whoever's at the door does a little more knocking, but I take my time, watching Jules until she's all the way out of sight. She closes her bedroom door with a slam.

"Keep your pants on." Whistling my way to the front door, I open it, casually leaning against the doorframe like I own the place.

"Can I help you—oh, hey, man." What's *he* doing here? I have Jules booked for tonight. "What are you doing here?"

"What are *you* doing here?" Beau's gaze goes downright stormy at the sight of me.

*Huh.*

I guess the clean-cut cowboy wasn't expecting me to be shacking up with the preacher's daughter while I'm in town. The friendly cowboy from the horseback riding lessons on the ranch is gone. This dude is pissed.

Are they hooking up?

"Just taking care of the little lady while her daddy's away." I offer him my most charming smile.

He's not disarmed by it. Funny. It always works. On women at least.

"Can I help you?" I ask, filling out the doorframe with my shoulders. I am bigger than him. Aren't I? Maybe we should whip out our cocks. I'm sure mine's bigger. "Was Jules expecting you?"

"Actually, she was."

Jules was promised to me for the night. Now I'm the one on an unlevel playing ground. "Really?"

"Really," he says.

"Why?" I ask.

"Because." He flashes me a grin of his own. "It's our date night."

## 6

# Jules

Running by the hall closet to get to my room made me remember what's in there and now I can't stop thinking about that...thing.

Maybe I dreamed the whole disaster. My dad says my mother had an overactive imagination, probably why she hightailed it out of this town, leaving us behind. Cedar Creek's loosened up their restrictive rules over the past few years but for someone like her, this town was closing in on her.

I forgave her years ago, but I can't pretend her actions haven't affected me. I try to keep a level head, to be dependable. I like people knowing what they can expect from me. Just like my dad.

And my dad would not have a dead body in this house.

My father wouldn't hurt a fly—even if he wasn't a clergyman. There has to be an explanation for this...package...that he's been hiding for who knows how long, then just busted out of the wall before he left.

Why would he need to tear it out of the wall now? Maybe it's cash. A long-forgotten stash of cash he suddenly remembered that will pull us out of this debt. That'd be great.

I'm just shimmying my jeans up over my hips when I hear Beau's muffled voice. Until the knocking, I'd totally forgotten about our weekly game night. I feel terrible to have double-booked Preston and Beau like this.

Maybe we can all get cozy, play Scrabble and drink cocoa?

I pop into the foyer and see the tension in Preston's shoulders warring with the narrowing of Beau's eyes. My visions of a peaceful game night dissolve. I need to get between them, and we can all laugh this off.

The lace of my sexy underwear moves against me as I hustle. I like knowing they're hidden under my clothes. I won't admit it to Preston but it's kind of nice not wearing my usual bikini panties and sports bra.

"Excuse me," I say, stepping out onto the stoop. "What did I miss?"

Preston crosses his arms over his chest, making his biceps look massive. "Beau here was just telling me that you'd forgotten all about your long-standing, every Friday night date night with *him*."

I stare daggers at Beau. "That's not exactly what Friday night is." I flash my eyes at Beau. "Is it, Beau?"

He crosses his own arms, giving a shrug. "Game night? Date night? Same thing."

Shooting an elbow into Beau's ribs, I brighten my tone. "Well, now that we're all here, why don't we all three get together? You know. Pop some popcorn—"

"You know we had a date scheduled for tonight, Jules." Preston leans against the doorframe, giving me his devilish grin. "But now it makes sense, Jules. You pretended to forget he was coming over. You're angling for a menage a trois, aren't you? I know you'd mentioned wanting one, but I didn't know you were *serious*. Tell me, how long have you been planning this little mishap?"

Heat creeps into my cheeks. "Preston. You know I did *not* say that."

"You don't have to be embarrassed. It's okay to ask for what you want. And I'd oblige you, of course. But." Preston's stone-cold gaze lands on Beau. "I'm not a man who shares well with others."

"You have nothing to worry about, then. There's nothing to be shared." Beau stares back. "I'm sure there are plenty of girls where you come from. You don't need to corrupt ours."

Icicles form in the air making the hairs on the back of my neck stand on end.

"Corrupt?" Preston laughs. It's a dangerous sound. "You were a lot more welcoming when I was getting a riding lesson from you. What changed?"

Beau says, "You know what? I don't think the reverend would like you here when he's gone. What did he call you again? The Devil, wasn't it?"

"Sure was. But anyone who's so much as smoked a cigarette in their lifetime is a devil in this backwards town. And she's twenty-five." Preston nods at me. "A full-grown adult. Capable of making her own choices."

Beau moves toward Preston.

Preston just stands there, cold as ice, arms crossed, leaning against the doorframe as casual as can be.

"Preston, you're exactly right." I put a hand on Beau's chest, stopping his move. "*She* is a grown woman who can make her own decisions. And I've decided that we're going to go inside and have a nice game of Scrabble."

These two men would rather poke their eyes out with a plastic fork than spend the evening playing a game together but it's their punishment for being so possessive over me.

I know neither one of them is willing to leave right now.

I get my way.

Preston stands, stretching like a panther and paces around the kitchen. He sees my copy of *Pride and Prejudice* and grabs it from the counter. He takes it back to his seat to read. They sit across the table from each other in silence, Beau staring stonily at Preston while I put some cookies on a plate.

Good. A little reading will be good for him—maybe that will keep him quiet for a minute.

I stir a splash of peppermint schnapps into their hot cocoa. Might as well throw them a bone.

I serve them their drinks and take a seat between them. "Isn't this nice?" I have a nice little laugh to myself, hiding it behind my mug.

"This does not count as our date." Preston slips a paper napkin from the table into the book to mark his place and plays the first word. "B-Y-E. Bye. As in goodbye, see you later, adios, ciao—"

"Okay, I'll mark down your points." I give Preston a wary look. He just grins back. I mouth the words, *Please behave.*

"My turn." Beau lays an L, O, and S tile, connecting to Preston's E. Then he adds an R. "Loser."

"I'll go next." I lay my tiles as quickly as possible. Going off of Beau's L, I play my word. "Love. See! We can all get along."

Preston tips his mug back, downing his drink. He puts the cup back on the table. "Can I get just the liquor this round, please?"

An hour later the board is covered in battling insults and a couple of my own personal best high-scoring words. I guess I was the only one really trying.

Beau yawns. He gets up early for his animals. He's always left my house by now. "Well, guys. That's game. Should we call it a night? Preston, I can walk with you home." Beau pushes his chair back, standing.

Preston leans back in his chair. "Nah, bro. I'm good. Jules and I need to finish the conversation we were having earlier."

I think of his hands on my ass, his fingers on me. My sex immediately clenches, dampening what should be the crotch of my panties. I stand to walk Beau out.

Beau gives Preston a forced nod. "Fine. G'night."

"Yeah. You too." Preston gives a half-hearted wave. He doesn't get up.

I walk Beau to the door. He hovers in the foyer, his gaze resting on the door to the hall closet. Why is he looking over there? Does he smell the dead body? I take a quick sniff. Nothing but the lemon cleaner I wiped the floor down with.

"Um, thanks for coming! I'm so glad we could all get together," I say. I open the door, stepping to the side and blocking as much of the hall closet from his sight as I can.

"This wasn't a get-together. Why is he here, Jules?" Beau gives me the look.

We've been friends our whole lives. He knows when I'm lying and he's asking me to 'fess up.

"I...well, I kinda like him." I think of Preston's deft fingers dancing over my sex and I want him to finish what he started. "And you have to accept it."

He gives me a long look.

"Beau," I say.

His gaze leaves my face, trailing over my shoulder.

Back to that hall closet, the current bane of my existence.

His eyes return to mine, lined with worry. "Jules, you going to be okay?"

He knows. Oh my God. He knows.

He knows and he's going to have me arrested. He knows and—

"Earth to Jules?" Beau's waving a hand in front of my face. "I said, are you sure you're going to be okay with him here?"

"Yes. She'll be just fine." Preston's deep voice rumbles through the hall.

Beau steps forward and with the movement of his boot heel, the level of testosterone in the room doubles. "Wasn't asking you."

"Okay guys." I clap my hands. "Beau, thanks for coming, I'll see you later. Preston, you can stay. But not for long."

I give a nod, happy with my delegation.

Preston gives me a *we'll see about that* look that makes my toes curl.

Beau tucks his tail between his legs and heads out.

By the time the door shuts, I'm exhausted. Too much masculine energy for one night.

"That was fun!" I say.

"I hated every minute of it."

"I know." I smile.

"Then why did you subject me to such torture! I mean, the kid was as boring as the game."

"He's not a kid. He's the same age as you. And I did it to teach you a lesson." I try to hide my smirk.

"A *lesson?*" His brow shoots sky high.

Whoops. My cockiness melts down into my toes at the sight of the impossible height of his brow.

"You wanted to teach *me* a lesson?" he repeats.

I squeak out a response. "Well, you were going all Neanderthal over here, acting like you owned me."

"If you want to see Neanderthal, I can give you Neanderthal."

Before I can respond, Preston's bent over, sliding a shoulder against my torso.

"Hey! Put me down!" I cry as he lifts me from the floor.

He tosses me over his shoulder like a rag doll. I'm laid over him bent in half, my hair hanging down over my face, my feet dangling behind me. He gives my ass a hearty slap. "Not till I'm ready, baby. Now where should we go first? Should we walk Beau home? We can probably still catch up to him."

He takes a step toward the front door.

"No way, Preston Bachman!" The idea of him parading me through town with my butt sticking up in the air—it's horrifying. "Don't you dare!"

He gives a chuckle so deep I can feel it rumbling through his chest. "Where should I take you then?"

"Put me down. Please!"

"One condition." He's moving closer to the door. He wouldn't really carry me through the town like this, would he?

"What?"

"You, Miss Jules"—he smacks my ass, leaving his heavy hand resting on my curves—"let me finish what I started before your cowboy friend showed up."

The sting spreads, a warm heat that travels straight to my clit, making it ache for his fingers.

"I might allow that," I say.

"Good. But first, you have to get these jeans off, don't you?" His finger dips into the waistband of my jeans, tugging at them.

Delicious tingles dance over my lower back where his skin brushes over mine. "I might allow that as well..."

"Well, let's go then." I laugh as he jogs us through the house and I'm bouncing against him.

We enter my room. I'm slightly embarrassed for him to see it. Since I've moved back, I've tried to make the place a little more grown up with sexy deep green velvet bedding and curtains, but yeah, my cheerleading awards still line the shelves.

He lowers me to the bed. My back sinks into the comfort of my familiar mattress, but there is no comfort for me. I'm full of electricity, my body tense, amped up.

My shirt's ridden up, baring my midriff. His eyes travel over my belly, hungry as they move up over my breasts, my peaked nipples showing through the thin fabric of my barely-there bra and tee. His devouring gaze heats my skin, makes me ache between my thighs.

Then, his eyes meet mine.

And all the heat, all the energy I'm feeling triples, his gaze hitting me straight in my soul. That night comes flashing back, the drama, the danger, then the moment he kissed me.

My first kiss.

I never told him that.

Then, when he touched me.

The first time a man *ever* touched me...

I can't tear my eyes from his, I don't want to even though a wave of emotions and nerves and fear and fantasy clench the muscles in my stomach, making my mind turn into clouds and my body into lava pooling over this bed, ready to burn it down.

He bends his body over mine, leaning his face closer to mine. His hand glides up the side of my face, cradling me in his big palm.

"Can I kiss you?" he asks.

He's already kissed me tonight. But I know what he's asking—we're bonded like that, barely knowing one another and yet knowing one certain part of each other better than anyone else does.

Maybe even...better than anyone ever could.

He's asking me if he can kiss me. Really kiss me. Not just with sex and lust and passion, which make for the very best kisses, but with our past.

The night that will forever tie us together.

"Yes," I whisper.

My eyes close as he moves closer. His breath heats my skin, the room now seeming impossibly cold, chill bumps rising over every inch of my flesh, but I know it's not the temperature of the room that sends shivers through my body.

It's the anticipation.

We're going back. To that moment. To that first kiss.

His lips meet mine and I'm back in that cherry red convertible, his hands on my body, his tongue slipping into my mouth, unlocking the secrets of passion that had only been mysteries to me up until him. Little snippets of overheard conversations in the locker room, girls' heads bent together whispering about their boyfriends.

Now his hand is running over my breast, cupping my curves. His hand moves lower, sneaking up under the hem of my tee. He's running his fingers so lightly over my nipple it makes me ache and throb with wanting.

His fingers find the button of my jeans, undoing it. He grabs the zipper, pulling it down so slowly I want to scream. He pulls back from our kiss just enough to croon, "Let's get these jeans off, shall we."

He nips my bottom lip between his teeth then he's back to kissing me, his tongue caressing mine. I lift my hips, letting him tug the denim over my curves. He leaves me, crawling onto my bed, his knees pressing down into the covers on either side of mine.

He leaves my jeans on me mid-thigh, looking me over. "Sexy, sexy girl." He grabs the hem of his shirt, pulling it up over his abs. He does that thing some men do—well, I've seen them do it in movies at least—where he pulls the shirt up and over the back of his neck to take it off.

Dang...that's hot.

I try not to be too obvious with my staring, but the man is a work of art. He sits there, shirtless, that damn cocky grin on his gorgeous face and lets me look. His skin is tanned, no doubt left over from his summer surfing. His arms are huge. He's got abs for days.

What the heck is he doing in *my* bed?

But now *he's* looking at *me*. The heat from the light in his eyes melts away any doubts I'm feeling as his gaze caresses my body. He thinks I'm sexy...

I move my hips a little to the side, showing him the curve of my body. He notices, gives a growl, and leans down, taking the thin elastic strap of the G-string that rides over my hip between his teeth. He pulls back and lets it snap back into place.

"Now it's really time to get these jeans off." He sits back up, grabbing them and tugging. I straighten my legs and he pulls them down my thighs, over my calves. He gives them a victory twirl over his head before tossing them to the floor.

He grabs the backs of my bare thighs, parting them. My legs move apart, cool air rushing over me. The panties are nothing but a picture frame, outlining the very place I want him most. I close my eyes, waiting for the touch of his hand.

But it doesn't come.

Instead, he nuzzles his face against my mound.

He's going to...go down on me?

## 7

# Jules

I try to squirm out of his reach. "Ah...I said no sex."

He holds tight to my thighs, locking me down on the bed. "This isn't our date. That's been moved to tomorrow at eight. And it's not sex. It's *cunnilingus.*"

I want to sink into the mattress and disappear when I hear him say the word cunnilingus.

As he speaks, the heat of his words caresses my sensitive skin. "And you said no 's, dollar sign, x' anyway. It's not even a word. I don't think that will stand up in court."

His breath is hot against me. Slick heat covers my sex. The cool night air and his hot breath fight each other for territory, resulting in a sensory overload.

Then, he laps his broad tongue against me, hot and wet, long and slow.

It feels warm and wet, making me squirm but in the best way. "Oh, oh…" A primal need takes control. I bury my hands in his hair, clinging to him, wanting to draw him in and push him away at the same time. My eyes squeeze shut tighter. My thighs fall fully open.

He licks me again and a thousand explosions of pleasure dance through me. My back arches and a sex kitten sigh escapes me. The sound makes him chuckle, his laughter vibrating over me.

I run my fingers through his hair. In this moment I'm nothing but the sensation of how it feels to have his mouth on me. With the tip of his tongue, he swirls circles around my clit. It starts to throb, wanting direct contact but he teases, circling hot wet circles around the tight bundle of nerves.

"Please," I moan.

"Please what, baby?" he whispers hot against my sex. "I want you to tell me exactly what you want."

What is it that I want? I read my body, searching for its demands. My sex clenches, empty and incomplete. And my clit aches so badly I need his tongue lapping it into comfort.

But can I really ask for those things?

His fingertips dig into the soft flesh of my upper thighs. "Come on, baby. Don't make me wait."

"I…I want your fingers, and…" My voice catches in the back of my throat. I can't believe I'm talking this dirty. It's so not me, and yet…

I've never felt more like myself.

I open my eyes, staring down at him. Sensing my gaze he looks up, offering me that sexy as hell grin of his. He's genuinely happy to be down there, he wants to please me. The knowledge gives me confidence like I've never known.

Holding his gaze to mine, the mellow sexiness I feel rolls from my tongue. "I want your fingers inside me and your tongue on my clit."

His brows shoot up. "Damn, girl."

"Now. Please."

He laughs, burying his face in my sex. He licks and laps his tongue, massaging my clit. A fresh pool of arousal slickens my entrance as he pushes a finger inside of me. He stretches me, adding a second finger to the first. I tighten around him, the fullness finally giving me some relief.

My eyes close, my head rolling back. "Yes. Just like that."

The waves of pleasure tear through my body. My skin prickles with perspiration, my head goes dizzy, his tongue doing things to me that have never been done. Gratification grows inside me, threatening to well until it bursts.

I'm going to come. I'm going to come hard. And it's going to be the biggest, best orgasm of my ever living—

The ringtone I've set for my dad's hotel room erupts from the pocket of my discarded jeans.

*Noooooooooooooooooo!*

Preston's perfect mouth leaves me. "You alright?"

Oh, did I yell that out loud?

Yikes.

The sound of the ringer beckons me. This cannot be happening.

But it is. I lean up on my elbows. "I'm sorry. I have to get that."

"You sure?" He wipes his mouth with the back of his hand, cocking a brow at me like I'm crazy. "Seems like you were—"

*God, don't say it.* I cut him off. "Yeah. Sorry. Can you hand me my jeans?"

I'm feeling selfish as hell...

My dad's calling me. He needs me.

And all I can think is…

*I'm going to fucking* die *if I don't come.*

He tosses me my jeans. "Poor thing. Another delayed orgasm." He gives me a diabolical grin.

"Tell me about it." I shimmy into my jeans and grab my phone. I've missed my dad's call.

I need to get Preston the heck out of here so I can call my dad back before he worries. I really don't need Preston teasing me in the background while I talk to my dad. I have a feeling he'd want to make his presence known and the last thing my dad needs is the stress of his little girl having a guy over while he's gone. Even if I'm twenty-five.

I toss Preston his discarded tee. "You've got to go."

With the flawlessness of an athlete, he lifts a hand in the air, catching the shirt. The man can make any ordinary task look sexy.

"I can't believe you're choosing to call your dad over my tongue. It's been known to make women cry," he says.

"I am going to cry if you don't get out of here. Go. Now!"

He slips his tee over his head as I usher him toward the foyer. I open the front door, gesturing for him to leave as I dial my dad's hotel room.

"Jules?" My dad sounds lost, far away.

"Hey, Dad!" I mouth to Preston *I'll call you tomorrow.*

"See you at eight, baby. Can't wait for our date," he calls out too loudly.

Pushing his massive frame of muscles out the door, I shoot him kill-daggers from my eyes, mouthing, *Go!*

"Jules, who was that talking in the background?" my dad asks.

"No one, Dad." Get going already. I frantically wave him away. "Just the UPS man."

Preston stands on my stoop and stares at me for a beat.

The tip of his tongue trails across his lower lip.

"I'll be your UPS man, baby," he whispers, his voice hot as coals. "With my cock all *Up in your Pussy Soon.*"

I'm going to die if my dad heard that. Preston walks down the drive, singing, *I'll be your UPS man, baby,* and whistling as he goes.

I slam the door behind him. "Dad, you there?"

"I'm here, honey. What did he bring?"

"What did who bring?"

"The UPS man. Did you get the package? It's probably the new hymnals I sent out for."

"Um…"

Did I ever get a package at my doorstep today. Six foot two of sexual energy and a mouth that can light a fire.

"Yes. It was just some girl stuff I ordered last week."

That shuts him down. "Oh…okay."

"Err…how are you?" I sink down into the sofa, wanting to focus on my dad. "How's the hotel?"

"Oh, it's nice enough. How are things at the house?"

"Quiet." Not lying. It's quiet now, right? Preston's done an excellent job of distracting me from my problem in the closet but now hearing my dad's voice the urgency of solving the mystery surfaces. "Dad, I need to ask you something—"

He interrupts me. "Mind if I go first, Jules?"

"No, that's fine. What is it?"

He sighs into the phone. "I need to ask you a favor."

"K…"

"I have a…project I'm working on. It's in the hall closet. And it's not coat racks."

Thank goodness! He's going to tell me what's in the closet. I scoot to the edge of the couch, ready to finally have the mystery revealed to me. "Okay…"

"And I need you to not go in there until I come home. Okay?"

I plant my palm to my forehead. Seriously? He's not going to tell me? Should I tell him what I found in there?

"Sure, Dad, no problem." I decide to file the whole thing in the back of my mind for now and respect his privacy. It's darn near impossible not to ask, but he'll tell me when he's ready. "How are the doctor's tests going?"

"Great. But…ah…" His voice sounds sheepish. "I actually wasn't entirely honest with you when I left."

"How so?"

"The doctors here, they're not actually doing any tests on me. It's a retreat, therapy, to help me figure out what's been going on with my body. There's one-on-one investigating into your psyche, I think that's the word they used, to find out what's really making you sick."

Psyche? This sounds expensive. I'm thankful for the deposits Preston's put in my account. I begin to think of his payments as a donation to my dad's recovery.

I want to reassure him. "Anything to get you better, Dad."

"It's pretty intense, three solid days of sessions with different professionals, but I'm really making good headway." His voice brightens with hope. "I'm already feeling better."

"That's really great. I'm so happy for you."

"Thanks, Jules. I miss you, though. Just two more nights here then I'll be home by ten on Sunday morning. Just in time to get ready for the eleven o'clock service."

He'll be out of town long enough for me to go on my date tomorrow night with Preston. I'll even have a little time in the morning to clean the house and decompress before he's back.

And pay our bills!

I smile into the phone. "Don't worry about a thing, Dad. I've got some money coming in—a little side project with someone from my past came up and it's doing well."

"With your fashion bloggerdoodle thing?"

"Yes." I think of the Versace dress hanging in my closet waiting for me to wear it tomorrow. "Fashion is involved."

"Well, that's just swell, honey. Whew. Really takes the weight off. I'm sorry you've had to help your old man out so much. It shouldn't be this way. I should be taking care of you—"

I cut him off. "You took great care of me my entire childhood, Dad. It can't have been easy raising a daughter solo. It's my turn to take care of you."

Tears choke his words. "I'm so lucky to have you..."

"Me too." I spare us the whole cry-on-the-phone-together moment. "But let's get some sleep now. It's late."

"Oh my—after midnight! I hadn't realized."

"It's been a long day," I say, thinking over the events of the past ten hours since Preston rolled into town.

His arrival seems like a lifetime ago.

"Love you, Jules," my dad says.

"Love you, Dad."

I hang up the phone and collapse against the pillows. "Holy cow. What a day."

Forget washing my face and brushing my teeth. I just want to read and drift off to sleep. Groaning, I manage enough energy to go to the kitchen table and get *Pride and Prejudice*. I think of Preston reading it, his dark brow furrowed, and I laugh.

He probably hated it.

I pull the chunky throw blanket I knitted from the back of the couch, curling up under it and opening my book. The napkin he'd left inside as a bookmark flutters out. I pick it up and go to put it on the side table, but the sight of inky black words scrawled over the paper stops me.

*You've never stopped tempting me*

My heart stills in my chest. My breath catches in my throat.

He's referring to the last line I read before I closed the book. He must have read it too, the one where Darcy is talking about Elizabeth and says, *She's tolerable but not handsome enough to tempt me.*

It's romantic and flattering and I know as long as I live, I will keep that napkin in a box in the bottom of my closet.

*But...never stopped?*

That's just something guys say, right? To be nice? To get *UPS*?

I run my fingers over his words. You've never stopped tempting me either, Preston. I read until I doze off, images of Preston sweetening my dreams, a smile on my face.

In the morning, I do my usual routine but I'm just counting down the minutes until eight o'clock. On my way to teach goat yoga at Beau's I pass right by Preston's. I walk super slow, craning my neck to see in his windows from the street but the curtains are drawn. His gold Land Rover isn't in the driveway.

I tutor kids in math, help Mr. Pierce with the loose wiring in his kitchen—I've become a Jill of all trades, I've found you can learn how to do anything on the Internet—and I walk Ms. Peterson's two teacup poodles for her.

She'll probably be the next one to move and leave Cedar Creek behind. She's out of town visiting her eighty-year-old boyfriend. They're getting married in a few months.

Always the bridesmaid, never the bride. *Am I right?*

I busy myself with cleaning the house, staying as far away from the hall closet as I can. I try not to check my phones too often. No texts from Preston. Or Dad.

At six o'clock I have a little bite to eat and finally let myself get ready. I take a long shower. Shave everywhere. Moisturize yards of skin. Blow out my hair until it falls over my shoulders in gentle waves, and put on a touch of gloss and mascara.

Now, for the moment I've been waiting for.

The dress.

## 8

# Jules

Preston shows up on my doorstep for our first official date at seven fifty-nine, another silver box in his hands. He's dressed way more casually than me, in jeans and a tee—and are those snakeskin cowboy boots on his feet?

I look down at my dress. "Um...am I overdressed?"

"Change of plans." He pushes past me, letting himself in. "I got to reading that book of yours last night and I thought of something better."

A trickle of excitement runs up my spine. *Oh, a Pride and Prejudice inspired date!* "It's my favorite. I can't tell you how many times I've read it. Did you like it?"

"God, no." Knitting his dark brow together, he says, "No offense? It was so boring, I almost stopped reading and talked to Beau."

I laugh. "It's so good! You just have to give it more time."

"No. Seriously. I hated it. And that guy, Darcy? What a jerk."

"He gets better," I say.

Preston tosses me a dark look. He's not convinced.

"You have to read the rest of the book."

"Not going to happen but I got what I needed from it." He lays the package down. "The book was so worn out I figured you must love the damn thing. The spine is cracked, and half the pages are dog-eared."

"Yeah. I'm bad about that. I really should use a bookmark," I say.

"You are bad." He moves to me, grabbing my hips and running his hands over my ass. "You should really be spanked for the way you treat books, by the way."

Heat melts to moisture between my thighs. Must he always turn me on like this with that filthy mouth of his?

He gives my ass a stinging smack. "Too bad we don't have time. We need to get going if we're going to make it." He moves away from me, making my body ache for his return.

Eyeing the new box, I ask, "What were your first plans?"

"The ones we had to cancel because of Scrabble?" He runs a hand through his hair. "You know, the usual. Helicopter ride, land on a helipad on top of a fancy hotel. Dinner at the hottest place." He shoots me an accusatory look. "I had reservations, you know."

God, that sounds amazing. I almost regret my impromptu game night. "Sorry about that. Can you tell me the new plan?"

He grabs my hand, leading me back to my bedroom. "I'll tell you but first you've got to get out of that dress." His eyes rove over my breasts and down to my hips.

I stare down at my baby, I mean, my Versace. She deserves to be shown off.

My fingertips glide over the silky fabric. "Can I ask, why do we have to change?"

"It'll make more sense if I show you. But first, the dress. I've learned from the Beauties that's the most important part of the date. May I?" He moves behind me, his fingers going to the zipper at the base of my neck.

"If I must." I heave a sigh.

The zipper moving down my spine feels like sadness. *Don't worry, princess, I'll take you out...one night.* Even if it's just to the Dairy Dream down the road, she's going to have her moment in the sun.

He helps me step out of the dress and to his credit, he hangs her back up with the respect she deserves.

"Wait right here."

He disappears from the room. I take the opportunity to throw on my old gray terry cloth bathrobe over the white lace bra and undies I've chosen for tonight. I mean, I know he's seen me in my undies, but I'm still getting used to the idea. He returns with another one of those gorgeous silver boxes like the ones he had Richmond deliver.

He cocks a brow. "Cute robe."

"I was cold." I feel a blush creeping over my cheeks.

"Sure." He holds the box out to me. "You're going to want to sit down for this."

I sink onto the bed, trying to feel grateful, trying to muster some excitement for what's in the box, but how can any dress compare to the Versace?

I take the gift from him.

The package is heavy on my lap, more weight to it than there should be for a dress. The shiny paper is cool and slippery under my fingers as I peel back the lid of the box.

Amethyst tissue paper hides what's inside. I pull it back, exposing a deep emerald velvet, as rich and bold as my bedding. Pulling the tissue back further, I expose gold satin, edged with a matching roping.

What is this? There're piles of fabric in this box and it just doesn't make sense.

"Preston, you bought me...curtains?"

His hand goes to his brow, pinching at it. "No, Jules. I did not buy you curtains to wear on our date. Will you just open it, please?"

There's so much material, I have to stand to pull the thing all the way out of its packaging.

I grab the edges of the braided gold rope and lift. It's so heavy...

A little gasp flies from my mouth.

It's a gown.

A proper ball gown.

"No way," I whisper, holding it up against my body. The gold bodice is outlined in the braiding. The green velvet meets the satin at the neckline, flowing into long bell sleeves. The velvet runs along the sides and back of the dress but underneath, just at my navel, gold satin peeks out from the dark velvet, pouring out and touching the floor.

I move to the full-length mirror, staring. My eyes are a deeper shade of blue, my red hair has never looked more elegant. Even my pale skin is glowing against this material. "I was born in the wrong era."

There's a chuckle from behind me. I'd forgotten all about Preston. I turn to him, still holding the dress up at my shoulders. "Oh, Preston. You have no idea..."

Are those tears welling up at the backs of my eyes?

How do you tell a man that you technically haven't even been on a first date with yet that he's made your dreams come true? That you've wanted a moment like this, a gown like this, an experience like this, your whole life.

"I read a lot, I mean a lot, of books with ball gown—I mean ballroom—scenes growing up. You have no idea…" I don't fully embarrass myself by pulling out my childhood drawings from the desk and showing him my sketches of fancy dresses.

"Makes sense. You did grow up down the road from a legit castle."

"Don't ruin this moment talking trash about the town, please?"

"Forgive me," he says. "Now are you going to put on that dress or just hold it all night?"

I debate for a moment. I want to wear it, of course I do, but I'm also content to just hold it and feel it and stare at it.

A slap on my ass makes my decision for me. "Hurry up. We don't want to be late."

"Where on earth are we going?" I ask, unzipping the back of the dress. Now I'm dying to wear the dress, but how will I fit in in the city in this gown?

He reads my thoughts. "I can't say. But I promise you won't feel out of place."

I glance down at his casual jeans and sweater.

He reads my thoughts again. "I'm going to the bathroom to change." A look of downright pain crosses his face, and he heaves a heavy sigh.

"What's wrong?"

"Listen, Jules. Just…God. I can't…just get dressed. Okay? You've got, like," he glances down at the gold watch he always wears, "ten minutes."

What's going on? Preston is always cool and collected. The man looks downright scared.

"Preston—"

"Just get dressed. Before I change my mind."

He leaves the room, closing the door behind him.

The worry I feel about Preston washes away the second the fabric touches my skin. The dress slips right on. It's got a built-in corset-like thing that pushes the swell of my breasts high and proud.

The design of the dress is genius, offering the drama of the gowns from that period, but with extreme comfort. Other than the weight from the thick fabric, it's as comfortable to wear as my cozy flannel nightgown.

I move side to side, letting the heavy fabric swish around my ankles.

He comes back in the most un-Preston-like outfit I've ever seen. What is he wearing? My hands go to cover my mouth, a giggle rising from my belly.

Don't laugh. Whatever you do, Jules, don't laugh.

"You better not laugh," he says, cocking his brow sky high. "Don't make me regret this."

"No, I love it! Let me see." I circle him, taking in the black trousers, cream-colored shirt, silk paisley cream waistcoat and the black silk tie around his neck. He's wearing a black morning coat with it, the tails flowing down his back.

On his feet are his snakeskin cowboy boots.

"They tried to get me to wear tights and some crazy-ass pilgrim shoes with this huge buckle on the toe but I told them no. And the top hat? You can forget it." He rakes a hand through his blond hair. "I had to draw a line somewhere. Sorry if I'm not totally authentic. There's only so much I can take, you know?"

I stand back and take him in. He could have been from another era too. I picture us dressed like this, children playing in the grassy meadow of our country estate. It turns me on. "You actually look...sexy."

"Enough. You don't have to lie."

"No, really. You do." But it's more than that. He looks...perfect. More perfect than any man has ever looked to me because he was willing to do something like this—go way out of his comfort zone and put on an outfit that makes him feel utterly ridiculous...

Just to make me happy.

"You look perfect." My voice drops to a whisper. "Thank you."

"It's nothing." His eyes travel to the gold-encased swell of my breasts. "But you, look at you. You look amazing. How do you make twenty pounds of fabric turn me on like you're wearing nothing at all?"

I'd normally brush off the praise, assuming he's just being kind, but the fire burning in his eyes tells me he means it. Besides, I've never known Preston to say something he didn't mean.

He's good like that.

The fire in his eyes turns to hunger. "Come here."

I go to him, the back of my dress trailing the ground like a bride's train as I move.

He takes me in his arms. He grabs the back of the dress, lifting the skirt, feeling its weight.

"That's a lot of skirt to get under." He presses a kiss to my lips. "But somehow, I'll manage."

The promise of pleasure courses through my body. The little bit of fabric he's lifting is tickling my lower back, teasing my skin.

I want more kisses, more caresses, but he's eyeing that watch. "Shit. We've got to go. The car is waiting in the driveway."

He grabs my hand, leading me from the room.

"I have to be back tonight. My dad comes home tomorrow."

"I'll have you home by midnight so you don't turn into a pumpkin. Just take a deep breath and let me take care of you. This is your night." He brushes a chaste kiss over my cheek. "Let's go."

The vehicle waiting for us isn't a helicopter, but it'll do. A driver sits behind the wheel of a pristine white Rolls Royce Ghost.

How do I, a Camry driver, know what fine piece of machinery sits in my driveway? Beau is just as obsessed with cars as he is with horses, and I've spent plenty of time listening to him talk about the latest models.

I stare at the sleek lines of the car. Soft blue backlights glow through the bars of the spotless silver grill. The white wheel covers are a maze of little rectangles. The car is a work of art.

"You like?"

I feel Preston staring at me. There's a light in his eyes I only see when he's made me happy. That light transfers down to my fluttering belly.

"Um...can I see the inside?" I ask, moving toward the car like it's a horse I don't want to spook. I can't imagine what it costs to rent.

"Yeah. I was thinking that's where we might ride," he jokes, grabbing the silver handle. He opens the door.

I peek in, giving a little moan of awe.

Ride in this car? Heck, I could live in the thing.

It's gorgeous, like nothing I've ever seen. The long dashboard is illuminated, tiny dots of a thousand stars twinkling. The soft glow overhead lights the cabin.

I peek in further. "Are those stars on the ceiling?"

More tiny lights sparkle over the velvety expanse of the interior roof.

Preston gives my hip a little pat. "Ah, Jules?"

"Hmm?" I ask. Oh my gosh, that leather looks so buttery and soft. I want to reach out and touch it, but I don't dare.

"You need to get in."

"Oh! Yes, I guess I do." Grabbing the sides of my dress, I lift it carefully, sliding into the seat. I rest my back against the warm leather. The seats are heated? Heaven. And *mmm*...I take a deep inhale... classic new car smell mingled with the smoky tobacco scent of the leather.

"Pull your dress in a bit?"

I look down. The very corner of the green velvet would have been trapped in the door had he not been paying attention.

"Thanks." I shoot him a smile, tugging my dress fully inside the vehicle. He gently closes the door.

A moment later, he's sitting beside me, pulling me into him and wrapping his arm around my shoulders. His clean, masculine scent mingles with that of the car. "We're quite the pair, aren't we?" he asks, looking down at our clothing.

"It's fun though, right? You can handle it for one night?"

"If it means getting to see these babies all night?" He reaches out, running a finger over the swell of the top of my breasts. "Hell, yes."

He teases, but I know he's done this—*all* of this—just for me.

If it was his pick, we'd probably be flying down the highway in some little sports car, me wearing a sexy little dress, him in his usual pants and dress shirt, hitting Paul's Cocktail Lounge on 6th or dining at Refinery Rooftop overlooking Manhattan.

Both amazing places that I'd love to go to one day but...

He's sitting here beside me in the comfiest luxury car he could find, dressed like a ball room god in his waistcoat and silk tie. And I'm in the very gown I used to spend hours sketching as a girl.

This moment just couldn't be more...*Jules.*

"So tell me about the boots," I say.

He looks down at them. "A gift from a friend. They're ugly as sin but I've gotten used to them."

There's laughter from the front seat.

"Driver," Preston leans forward. "We're ready for our drinks."

"Of course, sir. Right away." The driver even has a British accent.

I can only see the back of the driver's head, his hair covered in an old-fashioned driver's cap that I love, but there's something familiar about his movements—and his massive shoulders—as he exits the car with two cups he's taken from the front cup holders.

He goes to Preston's open window, handing two white paper cups through.

It's him—Preston's friend that delivered the boxes. "Hi, Richmond. I see Preston's roped you into delivering another surprise for me?"

"When he told me he was renting the Ghost, I offered to drive. I've been wanting to get behind the wheel of one of these babies all year. And I've got the right accent for it, haven't I?" He tips his cap at me. "Have a nice ride, love."

He slides back into his seat, slipping an earbud in one ear. He hums along to whatever music he's listening to as he pulls down my driveway.

Preston gives me my cup. It's warm. "Taste it."

I take a sip. My absolute favorite drink. Hot chocolate. He's mixed in some kind of liquor and it adds to the heat as it moves over my tongue. "This is delicious. What's in here?"

"It's Baileys. Sorry—I couldn't do the schnapps again." He gives a grimace.

"No. This is way better. Can I ask where we're going now?"

"Yep."

I wait for him to tell me.

He waits for me to ask.

I laugh. "Okay. Preston, can you *please* tell me where we are going?"

"We're going to the Meryton house," he says.

"Meryton house? Now why does that sound familiar?"

He stares at me, smirking, waiting for it to hit me.

"Meryton house? You mean where they held the Meryton ball in *Pride and Prejudice?*"

He nods. "You got it. Well, as close as I could get to a Meryton ball in the state of New York when we're not in the eighteen hundreds."

"What have you done?" I want to ask more but he's kissing me, stealing the questions right from my lips.

As he kisses me, my mind spins from the excitement of the incredible night he's giving me. It feels like ages ago that I was trying to whisper the word 'sex" into a phone. Even though that was only yesterday, now I feel like a woman, ready to conquer anything. I don't know if it's the dress or the car, or being in his arms, but I'm ready.

READY TO ASK FOR WHAT I WANT. READY TO TELL *HIM* WHAT I want.

I decide right here and now: tonight is the night my V-card goes. I'm giving him all of me.

## 9

# Preston

She pushes my hand away, tugging from my kiss. What's the problem? She clears her throat, pointing discreetly at Rich. *We're not alone,* she mouths.

Damn. Forgot about him. I should have gone with the Town Car, the smoky privacy glass would have separated him from us.

But I knew she'd love the Ghost. And she does. She runs a hand over the leather, sighing like she wants to wear it. "So soft." She grabs my hand in hers. "Tell me more. Please."

"When we get closer," I say.

If she was a pouting girl, she'd be sticking out her bottom lip. But she's not, so she tries to hide her disappointment behind a smile. "Okay. I can wait."

She has no idea the experience she's about to have. I'm sure she's never heard of The Primetime Period Players. It's an exclusive underground club I'd only heard about through Charlie. She's obsessed with vintage gowns and will do anything to get to wear one.

Without Charlie, I never would have gotten these tickets. I paid a hefty price for them and, judging by the light in Jules' eyes right now, it will be well worth it.

It's nice—to have someone to spend money on.

She stares out the window as we approach the gates. I stare past her at the woods I used to party in the year I lived here with my father when I was seventeen. I know we're both thinking of the same thing. It happened almost ten years ago to the day. I don't like the heaviness I feel, thinking about the aftermath of that night.

I push it away, choosing instead to focus on the memory of my fingers inside her. Heat rises in me, and I want to kiss her, to feel her lips on mine the way they were that night. She stops me with a question.

Her voice is somber and far away, a decade away, as she stares out the window.

I want to be in her thoughts. "What do you remember of that night?"

Her eyes grab mine. "You go first."

My throat feels tight. I pull my hand back, sinking into the seat. "Okay. I remember hanging out in the woods with the guys, throwing back some cheap excuse for whiskey."

She raises her brows. "Just guys?"

"There were girls there too…" I remember the light of the bonfire, tall orange flames, burning embers swirling in the air, guys giving each other a hard time, girls watching the guys, giggling. Typical high school kids kicking back after a football game. "I saw your car drive by."

"I was running away," she says.

"You were tearing down the gravel road, dust clouds billowing behind the tires of your little red car. The top was down, and your hair was blowing around your face. I thought, Jules Verduce? Out of the house after nine? That almost never happens."

"So true." She nods. "You jogged out onto the road, waving me down to stop. I didn't see you at first. I was crying too hard."

"You'd had a fight with Ava, right?" I ask. Ava was Jules' best friend, the princess of the town, living up in the Redmond Castle with her father.

"Yes. We were supposed to sleep over at her house after the game, but just like every other Friday, she ditched me for a boy. It was the fifth week in a row."

"I remember asking you where you were going so close to curfew. The gates were going to be closing in an hour. You said—"

She fills in the rest. "As far away as I can get. I didn't know where I was going but my dad already thought I was at Ava's. I was determined to spend the night away from Cedar Creek, show Ava that I could have fun without her. Seems silly now."

"Getting away from the Creek sounded damn good to me. I asked you if I could join you and you said yes. I didn't think you would."

She gives me a shy smile. "I guess I was feeling brave that night. I wouldn't normally let a boy I barely knew ride off into the night with me."

"I'm glad you did."

Silence falls between us, each of us thinking of what happened after we left those gates.

We chatted for a bit. I got her to laugh. God, I hated to see her cry.

We didn't know where we were going, and I hadn't cared. Every mile we put between us and Cedar Creek amped up the energy in that car.

Soon, we were singing along with the radio, poorly, and trading salacious stories about our friends.

I was telling her about Duke, the biggest kid on the baseball team and how he put peanut butter under his arms because he heard it would make him grow more armpit hair.

Feeling young and careless and free, I suggested our next activity. I put her in danger. And as long as I live, I know I'll never do it again.

I shake the rest of the story from my mind. I don't want to live in the past. I want to live in the now. I want to be here with her *now*. The way we are together *now*.

The connection between us is flawless. Sometimes it's almost like we can read each other's thoughts. But behind that easiness there's a constant tension, like dancing on a high wire, or a band stretched tight, ready to snap at any moment.

One look, one touch, and our easy friendship turns to passion.

We're getting closer. I see the iron gates rising between the trees. "Look." I nod at the window. Rich pulls down the long, pebbled drive. A streetlight glows every few feet and white luminaries light our path.

Jules scoots closer to the window. "What is this place?"

We reach a field where hundreds of luxury cars are parked. Rich turns off the road, parking the Ghost among them neatly in the next open spot. He turns and looks over his shoulder, giving me a smile. "Hope you two have a fantastic evening. I'll be here enjoying the car till you get back." His hand goes to the knob of the stereo, ready to test the sound system.

I help Jules from the car. We hear music blaring the second I close the door. I shake my head, laughing. "Rich and his damn Latin Pop. He can't get enough of the stuff."

"Where do we go now?" Jules grabs my hand in both of hers.

In the distance, I see pairs of partners, dressed in costumes like ours, headed toward the transportation that will take us up to the main house. "This way."

Her eyes go as wide as moons when she sees what's up ahead.

"Carriages? And horses?" She claps her hands together in excitement. Embarrassed by her outburst, she drops her hands to her sides. "Are we going to ride in one?"

"It's supposed to be an authentic experience. A real ball. Complete with old fashioned rides." I prefer horsepower to horse shit, but Jules is ecstatic, so I'll play Prince Charming.

She stares at the gowns of the women as they pass, her smile growing with each one. We reach the carriage with our number, 148, on a small number plate that's been tacked on the back. "Here, this is us."

The carriage sits on huge black wheels, so skinny I wonder if they can hold our weight. The bottom half is a lacquered wood, and black leather stretches up and over the top half of the carriage, forming the roof. At the front, there's a driver seated on a bench behind two massive horses—and he's wearing a white curly wig and those ugly-ass tights the lady at the store tried to make me buy.

He tips his boat-shaped hat in our direction. "Good evening, Guv'nor. And the lady."

I should be rolling my eyes at this guy, but Jules is so into it, well, I'd never admit it, but I'm starting to have fun. Anything for her. She looks so damn happy right now, it makes my chest feel all tight.

I give him a tight nod, helping Jules up into the carriage. I close the door behind us and draw the curtain. At least we'll have some privacy here. Two battery-operated "candles" light the inside. The walls and seats are lined with a deep red velvety fabric. Jules looks like a queen perched on her throne, right at home.

She loves it. "This is amazing! How on earth did they pull this off?"

"Money. Money can buy you anything."

She elbows me in the side. "Almost anything. Can't buy you love, can it?"

"It can buy you a date," I tease. "Almost the same thing."

She lifts a brow at me. "Don't forget the terms of our agreement."

"No seggs?"

She gives me a funny look.

"The recording you sent me." I shrug. "It sounded like you said eggs. Or seggs. I couldn't tell."

"Sex," she flushes. She looks me right dead in the eye, runs the tip of her tongue over her glossy lips and repeats herself. "I said *sex*."

"Hot damn. That's sexy as hell, baby. My little pearl's coming out of her shell."

I move closer to her, wrapping my arms around her. How long is this ride, anyway?

"I owe you an orgasm. And I'm going to give it to you. Right now." I rustle up yards of fabric till I find her bare legs. "But you'd better be quiet, or the driver will hear you screaming my name."

Her lips part as her knees fall open. She wants me to touch her. The only sound is the clip-clop of the horses' hooves as we move along the path.

"Do you want my mouth or my fingers?" I ask her.

"Neither." She holds my gaze.

"What do you want, then?"

"I want your cock. Now. I want it here. Right here."

*Holy shit.* My hands freeze at her waist. "Seriously?"

"Seriously." She looks like she's never been more sure of anything in her life.

"But aren't you afraid I'll hurt you or you'll bleed?"

*Do* twenty-five-year-old virgins bleed?

She rolls her eyes. "You don't have to worry about that stuff. Just because I'm a virgin doesn't mean nothing's been in there before."

Ah. Got it. My baby's got a vibrator. Nice.

"And what about the other stuff? I mean, I'm clean and you're—"

"Preston. It's all good. I've been on the pill to regulate stuff for years. Can we just get to the good part now?"

The girl is in her element. There's not a hint of shyness left in her. And I'm not giving her a second to change her mind.

I throw open the curtain and hang out the door, the night air cooling my skin. "Driver?"

"Yes, Guv'nor?" The man in the silly hat looks down at me with a willing-to-please smile. I think these guys work for tips. Good for me. I'll get what I want.

I whip my hand around in a circle. "Can you do a few laps for me? Me and the lady have a matter to discuss."

He tips his hat, a glimmer in his eyes. "Of course! Right-o!"

Anticipation turns to lust as I return to the carriage. Jules' eyes are shining, her face is flushed, and she's got a seductive smile on those full cherry-flavored lips that's just for me. She's back in my arms and my mouth is on hers. Her kiss is hungry and desperate. She runs her hand through my hair, tugging at the collar of my shirt.

I swipe my tongue against her bottom lip, pressing into her mouth. Her hand goes for my cock, timid but curious, her fingers grazing over the growing bulge. Suddenly, I'm finding myself a fan of the

Regency Era. There's something seductive about all the fine clothes, the candlelight, the velvet that surrounds us.

I kiss her, my fingers fighting the underskirts of her gown, wanting to get to that sweet, soft, warm spot that belongs to me. A swell of pride thrums through my chest.

This girl is pure perfection. And I get to be her first. The weight of what I'm about to do settles around my shoulders.

I pull away. "Wait. Don't you want your first time to be—I don't know—like, special?"

She laughs, a deep throaty sound that makes me harder. "What could be more special than this?" she says.

I tear off the stupid coat with the tails and toss it to the floor of the carriage.

I couldn't agree more.

## 10

J ules

He kneels before me.

I've wanted this for so long. My mind is set. My body is giving me every sign that I'm ready.

My heart gives pause. Part of me just wants to get this over with. I mean, not the sex, I want to enjoy that, but just the whole being a virgin thing. My little heart pitter-patters in my chest, scared to death that somehow letting this man between my legs in the back seat of this carriage will forever tie my soul to his in some kind of primal way that I won't be able to recover from.

But then I look into his eyes, feel the heat of his lips closing over mine, and I know with an earth-shattering certainty...

Our souls are already tied.

The carriage lightly bumps beneath us, the steady clip-clop of the dependable horses' hooves against the cobbled road the melody of our moment.

His kiss is possessive, his mouth moving against mine with hunger. His hands smooth up the sides of my thighs, battling with the crinoline of my dress. He wins, his fingers trapping the waistband of my panties. He tears his lips away from mine to lock our gazes as he slides them down over my legs.

He slips them in his pocket. The small act makes me giggle, the sound an eruption of nerves and excitement bubbling from my throat.

"A keepsake," he says. Devil's grin and then he's back at my mouth, caressing his tongue against mine. His hands find their way back under my skirts, fingers dipping into my slickness and dragging it up toward my throbbing clit.

I whimper into his mouth; his touch is more than I can take, and my hips shift away.

But he pulls me closer, locking in the back of my hair as he moves against me.

Warm waves of tension move through me. The massaging of my clit makes my sex ache and clench, empty, as a deep longing courses through me.

"Now," I say, gasping as I bury my face in his chest. "Now."

His hands make quick work of his clothing. I glance down, surprised to find myself blushing at the sight of his proud cock, standing hard and ready for me. It looks...huge.

I think over my limited glimpses of dicks. Is it supposed to be that big? An icy wave of fear washes through me.

It's quickly melted away by the heat of his hands on me.

I clutch at his shoulders, holding onto him as an anchor. He buries his gaze into mine, stroking my hair back from my face.

"You're mine." He brushes his lips over my cheek, trailing up to my ear. His breath heats my skin. "I'm going to *make* you mine."

My words are breaths. "That wasn't part of the deal."

"The deal is off." He nips my skin. "You're mine, Jules Verduce. And there's nothing you can do about it."

The word just falls from my mouth. "Fuck."

"See? I've already corrupted you." He teases my entrance with the head of his cock. His skin is warm and soft, yet hard at the same time and as it pushes against my tightness, I get wetter, helping him press into me.

My legs wrap around his waist. "Oh…my God." The feel of the head of his cock inside me—it's nothing like a vibrator or a finger. It's warmth and flesh and power. A feeling I've never experienced before, some kind of guttural submission, flows through me and I clutch him to me, curling my body against his as he stretches my sex, entering me.

A gasp catches at the back of my throat. He's so big, but somehow, he moves all the way inside of me. The fullness of him relieves the empty aching feeling but only for a moment.

I grow greedy, wanting, needing, demanding more. My fingers dig into his shoulders. I want him but I don't know what I want. Then he moves his hips against mine, thrusting hard.

A burst of pleasure erupts deep within my core. He pulls back, thrusting into me again. I lose my breath, perspiration dotting my skin and clouds numbing my mind until I'm nothing but the feeling of him inside me.

Hot kisses set fire to my neck, and he licks and bites his way down to the tender curve where it meets the top of my shoulder. Burying my face in his chest, I release a strangled moan into his shirt.

He rakes his fingers through my hair, destroying my curls and sending electric pulses over the back of my neck. He breathes hot into my ear. "There you go, baby, let it all go. Give yourself to me." His tongue licks flames against the lobe of my ear. "You know you belong to me. You always have, haven't you?"

I can't answer him. I'm too full of him, inside me, in my mind, in the very core of my being. I press my cheek into the warmth of his strong muscles and I just nod.

"Such a good girl." He grabs my hips, keeping me locked to him as he moves from his kneeling position to sit on the bench, pulling me up and over his lap as he rotates.

This is so much more than I thought it would be. Not only the sensation, the feeling of him being inside me, but the emotions. Being close to him like this…it makes my breath catch and my heart race. I'm perched up on him now, and he's deeper than before. He gazes up into my eyes as I stare down at him. I'm suddenly shy, on display, no longer hidden in the cocoon of his embrace.

He tucks a rogue curl behind my ear.

"Show me what you've got, baby."

My hands go to his shoulders. I sit, feeling his fullness. I don't know what to do.

The corner of his mouth turns up in a wicked grin as he grabs my hips underneath my skirt. His fingers dig into my flesh. His white teeth dip into his bottom lip and he won't break my gaze. He lifts his hips, pulling me down hard onto him as he does.

"Oh my." My eyes close, my head lolls to the side. He does it again, my back arching and my toes curling.

Wicked, wicked man.

With his encouragement, my body now knows what he wants. I'm shy at first, just holding his shoulders and feeling what it feels like to slowly move my hips toward his torso.

It feels good.

I move a little harder, a little faster this time, and the feeling deepens.

I let out a little moan. I catch a glimpse of him watching me. He's enamored, staring up at me like he's entranced by me, like I'm the most amazing thing the man has ever seen.

It's intoxicating, that look.

It gives me power, a desire to please him, a desire to enhance my own pleasure.

I grab his shoulders and, harnessing my newfound confidence, I ride him.

After all, like he said, I'm his. And if I'm his—he's mine.

I've never felt this sexy, this in control. I lean down, teasing his lips with a nip of my teeth. I move against him hard, then freeze, interrupting my rhythm, holding him inside, my muscles locked around him.

"My God, girl. Where did you learn these moves?" He gives a dark chuckle against my lips, then growls, "But you're not the one in control."

In an instant, he lifts me from his lap, setting me on my knees. My torso leans against the velvet seat, my breath coming in pants as I wait for what comes next.

He's behind me, the heat of the fronts of his muscular thighs pressing against the backs of mine.

His hands move my skirts up over my back. "This damn dress," he says.

He grabs the bottom curves of my ass where they meet the tops of my thighs. He pushes my legs apart. My knees slide against the floor of the carriage. My elbows dig into the cushion of the seat.

He gives my bare ass a slap. "God, you're sexy as hell, woman. Are you sure you've never done this before?"

I have to laugh at that. "I guess all that bottled up energy came out at once—"

But my words get strangled as his fingertips sink into my hips and his cock presses against my sex from behind.

He pulls me to him, bringing all of his hardness into me with one unyielding movement.

"Ah—gah!" My mouth hangs open as my waist bangs into the edge of the seat.

"You're so tight. You feel so good, Jules." He spanks me as he fucks me, his palm lighting a spark of fire against my skin where it lands. "You feel so fucking good, baby."

"Mmm..." I rest my cheek against my forearm that's pressed into the seat. My eyes squeeze tightly shut and I try to just breathe and take it but he's filling me up so hard and he's going so much deeper in this position.

It's making my core tighten like it will explode any second and there will be nothing left of me but little bits of Jules clinging to the velvet walls of the carriage.

He slides a hand up the back of my dress, smoothing it over my lower back as he rocks into me. "There's my good, good girl. Yes. There you are. Come for me, baby. Come for your man."

He's pulling me against him, demanding every ounce I can give him, his words making the tension grow tighter.

*I'm so close now...*

The carriage comes to a stop.

The driver's voice calls down from the top of the carriage. "We're here, Guv'nor!"

*Oh. Hell. No. Hell. No.*

I've missed out on too many orgasms this week. I'm not missing out on this one.

I press my palms into the velvet cushion, raising my torso from the bench. "Sir!"

"Yes, m'lady."

"Go around the block again. Now!" I bury my face in the cushions, adding a desperate, "Please."

"As the lady says," Preston growls.

"Righto, darling! We're off." The clip-clop of the horses resumes.

But the interruption is too much. Preston's doing all the right things, but I can't get back to that magical place.

"You okay, baby?" he asks, strain in his voice.

"Yes, it feels good, but I don't think I can come. The driver and the stop and—"

"Let me see if I can help, baby, because you're so fucking tight and you feel so good, you're killing me."

I bury my face in my hands while he fucks me.

"It's no use..." I say, my tone drenched with desperation. He's under my dress, reaching around, demanding access to me, pulling my belly away from the bench. His slick fingers find my clit and, "Ahh...ohh... uhn...um...."

*Game on.*

He builds his rhythm back up, building back that delicious tension in my core. His magical fingers dance over me, making me lose my breath. A heaviness stirs deep in my belly, a moan rising from that primal place.

It's coming. And I couldn't stop it even if I wanted to. "Oh fuck, Preston. Oh fuck." It's warm and wet and the feeling oozes through my body. I arch my back till it's scooped out hollow in a full cat-cow yoga move. My palm is damp and hot as it holds my weight against the edge of the bench seat.

My other hand reaches for his hand on me, cupping it and holding on for dear life while he milks the essence of being from my throbbing core.

"Yes, just like that."

As he groans, I feel him grow harder inside me. My sex wraps around him, clenching and drawing his climax nearer. I come first.

And the release is nothing short of a damn miracle.

I feel nothing and everything all at once. My body feels as if it's free falling, diving off a cliff, cartwheeling through a sky of tingling bursts of ecstasy. Is that too much? Another wave of climax tears through my trembling body, telling me no, this is as perfect a moment as I think it is.

His grip on my hips tightens. I'll wear the mark of his fingertip-shaped bruises tomorrow. He comes with the roar of a lion. Every carriage within a mile hears him. I feel his hot, wet seed filling me. There's so much, it spills out, running hot down my legs.

I like the feel of him in me and on me. I like him marking me with his cum. Marking me as his pretty little slut.

He collapses against me, and I fall against the seat.

"Shit, baby. I knew you had a little sexy goddess in you, but I didn't know it was all of you."

I laugh, brushing back my hair. I feel amazing, warm and loose and glowy, like I've had a bottle of wine. I'm drunk on him. I turn over my shoulder, catching his face in my hand and kiss him.

"We're a mess," he says, helping me up.

We clean up as best we can with the ironed handkerchief I grab from the pocket of his vest. When the driver stops, we exit the carriage, hand in hand, our clothes rumpled and damp, our hair standing on end, our faces flushed with perspiration and lurid grins like the cat that stole the cream.

We leave the carriage in a cloud scented of sex and lust.

And first times.

I'm so heady with afterglow it takes me a minute to register what I'm seeing.

*My God.*

"Preston," I gasp, tugging on his hand. "You've brought me to *Bridgerton.*"

## 11

# Preston

"What the hell is Bridger Town?" I ask. Doesn't she know from these woods that we're Upstate?

The forest is dense, thick with a tall wall of evergreens. The moonlight shines down, a bluish tint falling over us. It's a beautiful night.

"It's a show, well, actually it's a book, written by Julia Quinn but under another title—you know what, never mind." She wraps both of her hands around mine, leaning into me. "It's perfection."

Her eyes do that wide glowy thing that girls do when you've really hit a home run. Damn, she's so beautiful, and she's downright stunning when she's happy like this. I made her happy. I really like the way it feels when I make her happy.

I want to always make her this happy.

But her eyes are on the house. "Where are we?"

"Brighton Manor," I say.

A proud stone building that stretches the expanse of a city block. Its curving staircases go up the right and left sides, welcoming guests. A thousand twinkling lights are wrapped around the stair rails. Huge globe lights hang from the strong branches of ancient oaks, glowing over the grassy meadow.

"How...where...who owns this?" she stammers, slowly moving forward as she takes it all in.

"Five years ago, a few millionaire slash billionaire techie friends who were really into something called cosplay got together and bought this old mansion. They call themselves 'The Primetime Period Players.' The friend I got the tickets from said they were really into these things called Renaissance Festivals?"

"I know what that is. I went to one on a field trip in fifth grade. They made this medieval village, right in the middle of a town. Everyone dressed from the time period. There was a marketplace where you could barter for goods. It was all very real."

"Well, that's what this group likes. Apparently, they work their asses off in the city during the week, building their fortunes. And on the weekends?" I say.

She finishes my thought, her voice dreamy as we walk up the curved staircase. "They live to reenact the balls from the eighteen hundreds."

"Exactly."

So far, I like this place more than the description of the ball at the Meryton house in her book.

Dozens of couples, arm in arm, make their way up the stairs. It's a diverse crowd and the costumes vary in style, some more modern, some authentic. Others are made of brighter colors to complement warmer skin tones.

Some wear their hair like it's just another day in the city. Others wear puffy white wigs, or their hair piled high on their heads, feathers and flowers decorating their masterpieces.

A male couple walks in front of us, arm in arm, wearing matching shiny suits. They're dripping in gold sparkles from head to toe.

"I've waited all week for this," the man says to his partner.

"Same," his partner says. "And tonight the Victory String Quartet is making an appearance."

"Ah—mazing."

Overhearing the husbands, Jules stops dead, clutching my arm as if her knees have gone weak.

I wait for her to say something, but she's speechless.

"What is it?" I ask.

"The…Victory…String Quartet? No way," she breathes.

The massive doors are thrown open; a festive warm light beckons us. Music drifts through the air.

"How'd you get us in?" she asks.

"I had a hook-up from the family. Every week they host a ball, and a set number of tickets are sold to 'outsiders' like us."

The man in gold looks over his shoulder at me, turning to offer a hand. "Yes, we do. It's a pleasure to have you. Welcome."

His partner smiles at Jules while I shake his husband's hand. He eyes Jules' gown. "Gorgeous gown. Bona fide. Not everyone can pull off a vintage like you."

"Thank you." She gives my arm a tug, whispering to me, "Good job on the dress."

We enter the grand foyer. A man in a coat and top hat greets the couple in front of us with kisses on the cheek. "Oliver! Noah! So good to see you both."

He asks me for my pass. I hand him the two gold-plated cards Charlie gave me. He gives a nod and a welcoming smile.

"Enjoy your visit. The best view is from the top of the stairs. You'll want to go there first." He glances down at Jules. "Love the gown."

She gives a little curtsy. "Thank you."

"You've got a bit of fluff," he mouths to her, pointing to her curls. "Just there."

"Oh!" I help her pluck it from her tumble of curls. It's a bit of velvet from the coach.

*Whoops.*

We make our way up the curling marble stairs to a catwalk. We join the other couples leaning on the rails, staring down over the open ballroom floor, all waiting for something to start.

She pulls my ear to her mouth. "What are we waiting for?" she asks.

"I have no idea," I say. But then music drowns me out.

There's a heavy beat behind the instrumental as rows of people come from the wings, crisscrossing one another until they've formed battlelines like an army, rows of people going twenty wide and at least ten deep.

A cymbal crashes and they start to move in unison. Instead of the stuffy dances where partners circle one another, the entire crowd moves as one. Together they dip and clap, then jump and sway, arms to the right, arms to the left, moving in time with the tempo of a blend of heavy rock meets *Beethoven*.

And they don't miss a beat. Hundreds of shoes stomp on the wood floors with the music, then they clap again, twirling and dipping. I'm not much of a dancer, but I always give respect where it's due, and this is pretty amazing.

We watch in awe. Jules looks like a kid at Christmas. She's clutching my arm like if she lets go this will all disappear.

Like without me, she'll disappear.

At least, that's how I'm starting to feel about her.

With another crash of a cymbal, the song comes to a close. The crowd fanning around the edges of the dancers breaks out in applause. The dancers take a bow.

Jules watches it all with her hand clasped over her mouth. "I've never seen anything like this in my life," she says.

It's flashy and modern, the colors, the lights, the music loud and the bass thumping through my chest. I like it but it's nothing like the pages I read in her novel. "I thought it was going to be more like your book. Are you sure you like it? It's not authentic, I guess—"

She covers my worries with a kiss. "I *love* it, Preston. I love it." She leans up on tiptoes, kissing my cheek. We stand hand in hand, watching them set up for the next dance.

The band she's so excited about sets up their stringed instruments. Another group of dancers lines the floor. The room gets quiet, then music bursts through the echoing ballroom.

The lights dim and to the crowd's delight, the costumes of the dancers glow in electric greens and yellows and pinks. The quartet plays their hearts out, their full bodies almost dancing in tune with the notes they play.

The dance is fast and furious, punctuated with stomps and claps and shouts. Jules claps her hands to the music.

"Oh my gosh! Isn't this just the most amazing thing you've ever seen?"

A woman in a tux glides by, her silver tray filled with champagne flutes. Her short purple hair glows against the blacklights. "Would you like a drink?"

"Sure."

I take two flutes from her, handing one to Jules. Pomegranate seeds sparkle at the bottom of the glass. I take a sip. Dom Perignon. Nice.

I wrap my arm around her shoulders, pull her into me and kiss her cheek.

*My* girl.

My sweet, sweet girl.

## 12

**J**ules

Richmond pulls the Ghost into my driveway. I hate for the evening to end, but I need to get into the house. My dad will be home in a matter of hours.

"Preston, I can't tell you how much this night meant to me." I kiss his cheek.

He grabs my hand. "Come home with me."

"I can't."

"I have to go to the city tomorrow with Rich. I won't see you. Jules, stay with me. I'll have you home before the sun comes up." He's staring at me with those blue-green eyes, tempting me like the Devil.

I don't want to risk something going wrong and me not being back when my dad gets home. "I'm sorry. As much as I want to stay, I have to go." I pull away.

"Can't you just tell him the truth? That you're on a date and you'll be back later?" he asks.

Ah—the things guys don't have to worry about. Girls? We'll be fifty and our dads will still want to know where we are. "He's under a lot of stress. I don't want to put more on him right now," I say.

"You're a grown woman, Jules. You're allowed—"

I press my finger to his lips, stopping his words. "Please."

A mischievous glint flashes in his eyes. He reaches up, taking my finger from his lips and slips it into his warm mouth. He tongues the tip of my finger like he tongued my sex in my bed the other night.

I let out a low moan, pleading. "Preston…"

He takes my finger from his mouth. "Okay."

He leaves me, going to open my door.

I say goodnight to Richmond and thank him for the ride.

Preston offers me his hand and I take it, holding my skirt up as I exit the car.

Hand in hand we walk to my front door.

He leaves me on my stoop with a chaste kiss. "I don't trust myself to give you the kiss I really want to. I'd never leave," he says.

He waits to make sure I get in safely.

I feel like a princess collapsing on top of my soft bedding, my dress billowing out around me. Excitement from the evening flutters through my belly and makes me feel like I'm floating. I wrap my arms around myself as an anchor.

"I can't believe he did all of that. For me."

I'm sore between my legs, but it feels good, the kind of soreness that means something like when you've had a hard workout.

Or finally, finally had sex with a man.

I lay there, remembering every single magical moment from the evening, committing them to memory.

The next morning, slats of bright sunlight wake me up. What time is it? I stretch, patting my palm against the nightstand for my phone. Nine o'clock! Shoot, I slept in. My dad's going to be home any minute.

I spring from the bed and look in the mirror. My sexcapade hair is standing every which way from Sunday. I slept in the gown and it's frumpled and crumpled and oh geez, what a hot mess!

After stuffing the gown in the bottom of my closet—it'll need to be dry-cleaned—I jump in the shower and give myself five minutes to scrub the sex from me and wash my hair.

Wrapping a towel around myself, I take a closer look in the mirror. Do I look different now that I'm not a virgin? There is a pretty flush in my cheeks but that could be from the warm water of the shower.

But the sexy little glint in my eyes?

That's from Preston.

The moments from last night come rushing back to me like movie stills in photo frames.

His hands on me. His mouth on me. Him inside of me.

*Jules! Get it together!*

I throw on jeans and a sweater and rake a comb through my hair. Running through the house, I scrub away all traces of Preston. The clothing is tucked away neatly in my closet. I've put away our game of Scrabble, smiling as I tossed the tiles that spelled out their juvenile insults back into the box.

And the closet. Well, that's for my dad to explain.

There's nothing left to do.

Nerves start rising in my belly, thinking about the conversation my dad and I are about to have. What did the therapist say? Why does this secret in the closet have him so worked up?

I glance out the front window, looking for his trusty rust-colored station wagon. Wait...what's that...

*No. Freaking. Way.*

A white Rolls Royce is parked in my driveway. It looks just like the one Preston took me to the ball in. What is he up to?

I slip sneakers on my feet and go to the car.

I peer inside the windows. Same tan interior, same wood dash, same everything. I spot the two paper cocoa cups in the console.

It's *our* car.

But what's it doing here?

I grab my phone from my back pocket, dialing Preston.

"Hey, Jules. How'd you sleep? I slept better than I've slept in years—"

"Preston," I cut him off with my Sunday school teacher's voice. "What's the Ghost doing in my driveway?"

"Oh, that? Just a little token to remember last night by."

"You rented it again?" I ask.

"Baby, Bachmans don't rent. We own."

Own? "Preston—you...bought...this car?"

"Yep. And it's all yours."

*He. Bought. Me. A. Ghost.*

Holy cow. I can't even process this right now. "You can't buy me extravagant gifts like this." I have a ton more to say on the matter but there's no time now. "I appreciate the gesture, really I do. But you'll have to take it back."

He gives a low whistle. "That's gonna be a problem. They have a no-return policy."

"Preston." I've got to hide this thing. I try the handle. Locked. I smush my nose up against the glass, desperate to find the keys. I don't see them. "Where'd you put the keys? My dad's going to be here any minute."

"Let me see..." There's some jangling sounds and then he's back on the phone. "Shoot. You know what? Rich drove behind me when I delivered it this morning and when I got in his car, I must have slipped the keys in my pocket. I have them with me. And we're halfway back to the city. What are the chances of that happening?"

"*Noooo....*" I let out a groan, bringing my palm to my face. "If my dad sees that I've been gifted a car, he's going to ask questions. There's no way you can bring the keys here in time to hide it?"

"No," he says. "There's not."

And in his tone, I realize this isn't just a gift. This is Preston telling my father...

The Devil is back in town, and he's got your girl.

Preston is marking his territory.

Instead of peeing on my bushes, he's left a four-hundred-thousand-dollar car in my driveway.

"We are not done talking about this, Preston Bachman. I have to go."

I hang up, the sound of his chuckling ringing in my ear.

Think fast, Jules. Just make something up. It's not lying if it's saving your ass, right?

Of course, my dad pulls up right then in his old jalopy.

He climbs out of his station wagon, giving a low whistle as he walks around the Rolls Royce. "Pretty fancy piece of machinery. Where did this come from?" He glances at the house. "Is it Beau's? Is Beau here?"

He's always wanted me and Beau to be an item, but I've told him a hundred times that's impossible. My dad can't read between the lines.

I'm not going to lie. Preston is right. I'm a grown woman.

I say, "No, Dad. It's mine."

His brow furrows. "Yours? How is that possible?"

"It's a long story. One I'll tell you after you tell me yours."

"My story?" he asks.

"Yes." I throw my thumb over my shoulder, pointing at the house. "The one in the hall closet?"

"Oh, that." My father's shoulders sag, a paleness comes to his face. He suddenly looks ten years older. "Jules?"

"Yes, Dad?" He looks so sad, so worn out, it makes my stomach cramp with worry. What could he possibly have to tell me?

"Would you mind making us a pot of coffee, hon? We're going to need it."

I just stand in the driveway staring at him.

My dad doesn't even drink coffee.

Is this his version of going on a bender? What is he going to tell me?

"Decaf?" I ask.

"Fully leaded," he says.

Now I'm really scared.

We go into the house, and I brew a pot of my favorite, a smooth, medium blend, lacing his with a heavy dose of cream and sugar.

I take mine straight, though I don't even think I can drink it. My nerves are shot, but I want the comfort of the warmth of the mug in my hands. Something solid to hold onto when I feel like my life is about to be turned upside down.

We sit across from one another. He rests his arms on the table, crossing and uncrossing them. He takes off his glasses, perching them on the top of his head. Puffs of his gray hair stick out on either side of the lenses. He pinches the bridge of his nose between his fingers, exhaling a gust of air.

I reach out, putting a reassuring hand over his. "Please. Dad. Just tell me."

Finally, he looks at me. There's a weight and a sadness in his eyes. He always carries it there, ever since my mother left, but now it seems even more...sad.

"Oh, Julie Belle." The sound of his old nickname for me makes me wish for simpler times when the two of us would solve our problems with ice cream at the Dairy Dream. "I don't even know where to start."

"Start with your trip. The doctors. What they did for you, what you all talked about."

"Like I said, it wasn't clinical, blood testing and such. A few weeks ago I got to talking with Erin after the church picnic. I was telling her about my symptoms, the headaches, the brain fog, that weird feeling in my chest, the forgetfulness. I told her about all the different doctors I went to, the EKGs, the CAT scans, the vials and vials of blood they took. And how they never found anything. And do you know what she said?"

I want to laugh. He always asks me if I know what the person says when he knows I have no idea what they said. But this doesn't seem like a laughing matter.

"What did Erin say, Dad?" I ask. I take a sip of my coffee just to have something to do with my pent-up energy.

"She said the problem isn't with your health. It's with up here," he points to his temple, "and here." He puts his hand over his heart. "And you know what? She was right."

"So, Erin told you she thought your illness was caused by something... psychological?" I ask.

"Yes. She gave me this pamphlet for this great retreat. A spiritual healing facility but not just that new age mumbo jumbo stuff, there were licensed psychologists there as well. They helped me do a deep dive into my past—our past, really…"

"Like what?" The seconds tick by like hours. "Dad. Tell me."

"I've not been completely honest with you." His eyes hold mine and I have to look away. There's too much heaviness there for me to bear.

There's only one subject I know of that makes him this upset.

"This is something to do with Mom." I look down at the dark pool of coffee in my mug, twisting the handle left then right. "Isn't it?"

"Your mom was... troubled, Jules."

"Dad, we've been over this before. Just because Mom left, that doesn't mean she was troubled. Cedar Creek was just too small for her. She had a big personality, big dreams. This town just wasn't right for her."

"That wasn't it." He shakes his head. "I'm telling you, it wasn't."

His voice has a tone in it I've not heard before. I take note, scooting to the edge of my seat. "What are you trying to tell me, Dad?"

He leans his elbow on the table, rubbing his forehead between his forefinger and thumb. He looks ten years older than when he left. "I'm trying to tell you that your mother was sick."

"Sick? What kind of sickness did she have?"

"She battled with her mental health. Only, I didn't have the capacity to recognize what was going on at the time. I just thought she was, I don't know, a free spirit, or just felt things deeper than other people..."

His words trail off and I think back to the clips of memories I have of my mother. There aren't many, but there's an intensity to them. A technicolor larger-than-life circus kind of quality to them.

My mom taking me to the county fair, us coming home covered in sticky cotton candy, our arms full of oversized stuffed animals we'd won.

We're collecting wild mushrooms in the forest. She'd read a book on edible plants and was convinced we could feed ourselves from the woods. We combed the mossy forest floor until our legs ached and the moon hung high and full in the inky night sky.

Skipping kindergarten to spend the day making blanket forts in the living room, stringing fairy lights above our heads and eating boxes of cookies until I got sick.

I threw up all over my pink blanket.

My dad gives me silence, sipping his coffee while letting me comb deeper through those memories. When we'd gotten back from the day at the fair, I remember my dad's worried face watching us from the window. Him carrying me to bed in his arms.

He washed my face, helped me dress, then pulled the covers up to my chin, kissing me goodnight. He was always the one to tuck me in at night.

*Wasn't he?*

An inkling of realization tickles the back of my mind. "She didn't tell you we were going to the fair that day, did she?"

He shakes his head. "No. I was worried sick. She'd taken you from the school early and just took off. I had no idea where you were or when you'd be back."

And the mushrooms...what was a child doing in the woods sunup to sundown, looking for edible plants. And was my mom even capable of detecting which were safe for her little girl...

I finally drag my eyes up to meet my father's. "The day in the forest?"

"Oh my. That day." The color seems to drain from his face. "If I'd found you one minute later, you'd have eaten one of those—never mind." His hands clench into fists and he gives a shudder. He shakes his head. "You were safe and that's all that mattered."

A queer feeling comes over me, a wave of nausea that has a high heat to it, making me feel feverish and sick all at once. "And skipping school. Eating nothing but cookies all day to the point of getting ill. That was her too, wasn't it?" I ask.

"Yes," he says. "She stopped letting you go to school. And you loved that school. You and little Ava went together every day."

"Why did she pull me out?" I ask.

"She started to have visions, or premonitions, I've forgotten what she called them. She said you were meant for greater things, and that she knew you would change the world when you grew up but if you stayed in that school, it would make you small. I just thought she was lonely with you gone three days a week. I let her keep you home. But then...things got worse."

He can't meet my eyes.

My voice is barely a whisper. "What, Dad? Tell me."

Finally, he drags his gaze up to mine. What I see there makes my stomach flip. He says, "She got violent."

I think of my mom's cold, soft hands, her billowing cloud of beautiful auburn curls, the scent of her lavender perfume. She was a gentle spirit.

I shake my head, unable to believe this of her. "I don't remember her being violent."

"She had manic episodes, the ones like the day at the fair and the day in the woods. They were always followed by days spent in bed, or in the blanket forts with you. I finally convinced her to see a doctor. She agreed because she was upset about the times she was down. She wanted her life to be that high-energy mania, every day." He runs a hand over his brow. "I just wanted to get her help, get her balanced, you know?"

"Right." In his shoes, I would want the same.

"Well, the doctor put her on antidepressants. They worked great at first. She felt better. Her moods were more stable. But then, a few weeks in, she started to lash out. I'll spare you the worst of the details, but I was worried for your safety. I had Ava's family take you for a few weeks while I tried to get help—"

"I remember," I say. My dad dropped me off at Redmond Castle with my little red suitcase on wheels. I stayed more nights in a row than I ever had before. "Ava and I called it our 'summer sleepover.'"

"Yes," he nods. "The darkest time, it was then. I was so grateful you weren't home for that."

"Did you get her more help?" I ask.

"I tried." He shakes his head. "But I was too late."

*Too late?*

My mom was violent. Prone to manic episodes. Did my mom…hurt someone? Oh my God. The body in the closet. My mom killed someone, and my dad covered for her.

Then she ran off.

That has to be what happened.

I stare at my dad. A total stranger stares back at me.

## 13

# Preston

It's Jules. I can barely understand her through her tears. "Preston. Please. Please."

Is she okay? Has she been hurt? My heart lurches into my throat. "Jules. Tell me. Now. What happened?"

"My dad. He's been keeping secrets from me and that—thing—in the wall, the thing I found in the hall closet, I think it really is a dead body—"

I cut her off. "A dead body? What are you talking about, Jules?"

She's either not heard me, or not coherent. Her words keep flowing. "And I've been sleeping here with it, and I don't know for sure if my mother was a murderer but I've been sleeping on the other side of the wall. Next to. A dead body. For years." She bursts into a fresh set of wails.

I have no idea what she's talking about, but Jules doesn't freak out over nothing. She found a dead body in her wall? I just need to be with her now. "Jules. I'm on my way. Where are you? Where's your dad?"

"My dad only told me part of the story. Then he got this migraine and had to lie down and I just went outside and called you and when I heard your voice, I just broke, I just lost it."

"I'm coming right now. But I don't think you should be alone till I get there." And it doesn't sound like her dad is in any shape to sit with her. I think of the one person I can trust her with until I get there.

"Okay..."

I'm going to have to call the damn cowboy. "Jules, stay on the line with me. I'm going to get Beau to come and get you. Stay with him until I get there."

"Okay, okay..."

"Take a deep breath," I say. "And pack a bag. You're staying with me until we get this sorted out."

"Okay...okay," she says again.

"Sit tight, baby," I beg.

I put her on speakerphone, crooning sweet, calming words to her while I text Beau.

*Hey*

*Somethings up with Jules and her dad*

*I don't have much info but she's upset*

*Can you grab her from her house and stay with her at yours until I can get there*

*I'm on my way from the city*

*I'll text when I'm closer*

He responds just like I assumed he would. No long string of questions, just two lines.

*Got it*

*On my way*

They're waiting for me by the bridge. The second I lay eyes on Jules, I get that funny tightness in my chest and I feel short of breath. The world feels jumbled, yet finally all is right with it at the same time. The first time it happened I thought it was a heart attack.

Now I take it for what it is.

I'm falling in love.

I park the car and go to her.

"Preston." She falls into my arms, burying her face in my chest. It makes me feel like twice the man I am. "Thank you so much for coming."

I kiss the top of her head, smoothing her hair back. "Always."

I catch Beau's eye. "Let me get her settled in the car. I'll be back to get her bag."

I wrap my arm around her shoulders, getting her cozy in the car. She shoots me a grateful smile just before I close her door. My chest fills with warmth.

Jogging back over to Beau, I hope for a quick exchange.

He hands me her bag. "Nice car." He nods to the black BMW iX M60 I recently bought. "Six ten horsepower on that thing. Didn't think they were off the showroom floor."

"I know a guy," I say, slinging the bag over my shoulder. The all-electric SUV can hit 60 mph in 3.6 seconds flat. Too bad this guy and I are on not-so-great terms—he'd love to poke around in my garages. "Less flashy than my other cars but I thought Jules would like this one best."

He narrows his gaze. "So you guys are, like, an item?"

"Yes. She's my girl." Damn, saying those words feels so good, especially saying them to him.

His brow furrows like he's got some kind of claim on her. "You taking good care of her?"

"Yes. Very good care of her. Thanks for asking," I say.

"You sure?" he asks.

"Jesus, man." Can we just get our cocks out already and see whose is bigger? "I've got to get going. I want to get her home."

"To the Bachman Village?"

"Yes. *Home,*" I say.

"Lots of shady shit goes down over there. That's what I've heard." His blue eyes go icy. "Lots of ex-cons working for you guys, right?"

My fingers clench into a fist. Cool it, Preston. Don't let him piss you off. Besides, he's not wrong.

The way he's eyeing me…how much does he know?

"That's how we started but our business is legit now." Like 99%. Okay, maybe 75% legit. But we'll get there. We're a work in progress. "Don't worry yourself over it."

"I'll never not worry about Jules."

"Me either." I give him a wave. "But seriously, man, we've got to take off. Thanks for staying with her."

"Didn't do it for you—*man.*" He turns on his bootheel and walks away.

Asshole.

I slide into the BMW, putting the unpleasant conversation behind me. All I care about now is taking care of Jules. She's got her hoodie balled up, using it as a pillow between her and the window.

"Here." I reach over her lap, sliding her seat back down so she can rest. I pull the seat belt over her, buckling her in tight. "Rest."

She's in shock. Should I take her to a doctor? "You okay?"

"I'm fine. I promise. I just need a moment to process everything. You know? When you find out the past isn't what you thought it was…your whole world turns upside down." She gives a heavy sigh.

I just want to make everything right in her world.

I grab her hand, bringing it to my lips. "I'm going to take you home. Get a bath going for you. And while you soak, I'm going to cook you dinner."

She rests the back of her head against the headrest. "Mmm…that sounds nice."

I'm not sure what to say. It's not every day your girl calls you crying because she thinks her mom's a murderer and the victim's body is hidden in the closet. "Do you want to…talk about it?"

"Not really. Not now. But I'll fill you in, I promise. Thank you for understanding."

Her phone rings. "Ugh, it's my dad. I'm not ready to talk to him." Her fingers fly across the screen.

"What did you tell him?" I ask.

She reads me the messages. "Staying with a friend. Need some time to process. I'll call you soon."

"A friend, huh? Is that all I am to you?" I tease.

She laughs, nudging me with her elbow. "No, but there's no way in heck I'm telling my dad we're dating." She goes shy on me. "I mean, we are dating, right?"

"We'd better be. They don't let anyone who's not family stay at the Village unless it's serious."

"Are we?" She sneaks a glance at me. "Serious, that is?"

"Hell yes, we are." I give her thigh a squeeze. "You're mine, baby. *All* mine. And when you're my girl?"

"Yeah?"

"You do what I say or you get in trouble. Do you understand?" I give her thigh a sharp little pat.

"Yes, sir," she laughs.

She has no idea how hard it makes me to hear those pretty words roll off her tongue. "Good. Now rest."

She snuggles down against her hoodie. Sleep is what she needs after the day she's had. Soon, she's drifting off. I leave my hand on her thigh. Every so often I glance over to stare at her. She gives a muffled little sigh. Freaking adorable.

God. She's beautiful.

We're just passing the shops that line the walls of the Village when the sound of my ringing phone fills the cab of the car. Damn. Forgot to turn off the ringer. I silence it but it's too late. Pulling up to the curb, I cut the engine.

She's stirring beside me. Stretching and yawning. "Where are we?"

"We're just outside the Village." It's Rich. "Sorry, I've got to take this. Sit tight."

I step out of the car, keeping my eye on her. She's cute, sitting up and taking in the brownstone shops with wide, bright eyes. I can tell by the light in her face, she loves it.

"Rich, what's up?" I ask.

"Hey, mate. You're not going to like this. Rockland wanted me to pass on a message."

Visions of my quiet evening at home disappear. "Alright?"

"He knows you have a visitor but he's still hoping you're going to make it to the monthly family get-together tonight—and you know what hoping means."

"We'd better get our asses there?"

"Exactly," he laughs.

I groan. "Seriously?"

"Yup. I'm on my way to the rooftop to get the bar in order now."

I run a hand through my hair. "I was hoping for a quiet night in. No such thing with the Bachmans, is there?"

He gives a laugh. "Nope. 'Fraid not."

I hold back a sigh. "I know he wants me there so he can meet Jules. How'd he even find out she's in town?"

"Oh," he laughs. "You know how."

"Tess?" I ask.

Rockland's got a redhead of his own. A feisty wife with a bit of a temper and a penchant for gossip. She's the head of the Beauties and nothing—I literally mean not one thing—happens without her finding out about it.

"Yep. I guess Charlie told her about the tickets to that crazy dress-up party I drove you to—"

"Don't call it that," I say with a groan. "If the guys find out I almost wore tights, I'll never live it down."

He laughs into the phone. "You looked posh! Anyway, so the birds got to talking and then a few more joined them, and they were all like, 'Oy! This must be serious. Preston never takes a girl out more than once.' And then they really got going and someone saw you hightailing it to the Creek and got suss."

"Suss?"

"Suspicious, mate. Anyway, the party's at eight. Her dress and shoes are already hanging in your closet, courtesy of Miss Charlie."

I glance at Jules. She's sitting tight but looking more curious, staring at me through the glass. "I've got to go. Thanks for the heads-up." I slide into the car, hating to break the news to her that our night alone is canceled.

"Who was that?" she asks.

"Rich," I answer, just as his electric blue Lambo comes flying past us. "There he is now."

He blares the horn, waving at us as he blows by, Latin pop music blaring from his rolled down windows.

"A Lamborghini? Rich is rich as sin," she says, laughing.

*Rich as sin.* I like that. I'm going to have to use that one.

"What did he want?" she asks, craning her neck to watch him zigzag through traffic.

I pull back onto the street, going about fifty miles an hour slower than my friend. I've got precious cargo.

"How are you feeling, you know, after all this family drama you've had today? You kind of hoping for a quiet night in?" I ask. Surely Rockland will understand if I tell him what my girl's been through today. Maybe we can skip it…

"Honestly, I'm up for anything." She shrugs. "A distraction from my crazy life would be good."

"If a distraction is what you're looking for, you're in luck." A rooftop gathering overlooking the city with about a hundred curious Bachmans milling around her, a full bar and never-ending trays of heavy appetizers from The Bitch'en Kitch'en, our current favorite tapas place, should do the trick. "We do this family get-together every month. And it happens to be tonight at eight."

"Like, a party?" She looks at me with wide eyes and raised brows.

"Party might be an understatement." We cruise by Daughtry's Clothing and the Bachman's jewelry store. We're almost to the gate. I want to admit something to her I haven't yet. "And a few people want to meet you, because...well..."

"Well what, Preston?" she asks in her Sunday school teacher's voice.

My throat tightens. I clear it. "I've never brought a girl home before. You're the first."

"Seriously?" Her eyes go wide, a slow smile spreading over her pretty face. "Really, truly?"

"Yep. I guess we were each other's firsts in a way." Preston, that's so sappy. Get a grip.

She goes all gooey on me. "Aww... you're so sweet."

I change the subject. "We'll have to get ready pretty soon."

She looks down at her jeans. "I don't have anything to wear."

"Baby." I toss her a look. "The Beauties have this kind of thing covered. They'd never do you wrong like that, inviting you to a party with nothing to wear. Trust me."

The black security box recognizes my car, sliding the gate open for us. We pull up to the second gate. It opens as well, revealing the Village.

She scoots to the edge of her set. "Oh my God. It's real."

I laugh. "Yes. It sure is."

She gives a little gasp. "I mean, I knew it had to be, but seeing it, all hidden back here right in the middle of the city? It's incredible."

We own the brownstones that surround us, forming a protective square around us like the bailey of a castle. There's a grassy meadow in the center dotted with tables and couples dining in the sunshine. Tree-lined streets with sidewalks and rows of three-story townhomes greet us.

"It's gorgeous. Look at how each home is painted a different color and oh, I love that yellow flower wreath, how adorable!"

This girl was born to be a Beauty. She loves our Village. Wait till she sees the dress. Knowing Charlie, it'll be perfect.

Jules wants the full tour of my place. The outside is gray and black, the inside white and navy. The décor is lacking but my modern furniture has clean lines, and my leather couches are buttery soft.

She glances around. "Nice."

"But?" I say, taking her into my arms.

She wraps her arms around my neck. "No offense. But it could use a woman's touch."

"None taken." I lean down, grazing her lips with mine. "I wonder if there's a woman up for the task?"

She flushes, a shy smile crossing her face. "Maybe?"

I lean down, my lips against hers. "Well, I know just the woman. And right now, she could really use a man's touch."

## 14

**Preston**

Carrying her up all three flights of stairs to my bedroom is just the warmup. The real work starts when I get her clothes off. She giggles as I slide her to her feet.

"Gosh, you're strong." She runs her fingers down my biceps and over my pecs.

The feel of her light touch does insane things to me, tightening my core and flashing heat through my stomach. I don't brag that I can bench-press her weight. But I can. Instead, my fingers go to the button of her jeans.

Pushing them down over her hips, I find her bare underneath. "No panties? So naughty."

"I didn't have time this morning. It's really all your fault." Her arms above her head, she stretches, showing off her body. "Someone kept me up oh so late and then there was an unexpected vehicle in my driveway?"

"Mmm. I like. I'm going to have to buy you more cars." I leave her jeans hanging at her knees and smooth my hands over her bare ass. God, her skin feels so good. Bumps rise on her flesh and she melts into me, demanding kisses.

I swipe my tongue over her bottom lip, giving her ass a little smack. "Let's see if you forgot your bra too."

Slipping my hand under her sweater, I travel the length of her trembling torso. A moan leaves me the moment my hand comes in contact with her bare breast. I cup it against my palm, the feeling closer to heaven than I deserve.

I palm the fullness of her curves. Her sweet nipple grows taut under my touch. I need the tight little bud in my mouth. Pushing up her sweater, I bend a knee, bringing her breast to my lips.

"Oh, Preston," she sighs as I cup and taste, teasing her nipple with the edges of my teeth. Pulling at her shirt, she lifts her arms, letting me free her of the sweater.

Tossing it to the side, I take a moment to just look.

Pink blotches circle her cheeks, her eyes shine. She bites at her bottom lip as I stare. My heated gaze makes her nipples peak further, wanting more of my touch, her breasts heaving with deep breaths of desire.

I pull her to the bed, leaving her jeans around her knees. She's on my lap and I'm teasing her breasts. Her arms wrap tighter around my neck as I kiss her. I stare at her reflection in the full-length mirror across from my bed.

"Look," I say, watching her face.

The deep flushing of her cheeks comes, just as I knew it would. "Oh!" At first, her arms fall from my neck, wrapping around her breasts to hide them from view.

"Don't be shy," I say, taking her arms and moving them away, exposing her breasts to my gaze in the mirror. "I want to see."

She drops her gaze, unable to look at herself in the mirror. I tug at her jeans, discarding them on the floor. I'm fully clothed. She's fully nude. And all mine.

I lean back on the bed, pulling her over the center of my body so her ass is cradled between my legs, the hardness of my growing erection pushing into the naked crack of her ass. Her back rests against my chest. Stretching my legs out in front of me, I balance her legs over them.

The backs of my fingers drag over the sides of her ribcage. I take her arms, stretching them over her head and wrapping them around my neck. "Stay just like that, baby. Keep your hands right there."

She obeys, locking her fingers together behind my neck. Her breasts rise and fall with her shuddering breaths.

Running my fingers down the backs of her arms, I find her chin, cupping it and raising it until her gaze is locked on mine in the reflection of the mirror. "Don't take your eyes off me," I say.

Parting her thighs, I slip my fingers into her slickness, rubbing over her clit. As a shiver shoots through her, she lolls her head to the side with a moan, closing her eyes.

My fingers leave her sex. I give her pussy a sharp spank.

"Oh!" Her eyes fly open and she jumps on my lap, her ass landing back down, sending warm waves through my cock. "What was that for?"

"I said, your eyes don't leave the mirror." I take her arms, wrapping them back around my neck and settle her back into place. "Now be a good girl and do as I say."

She gives a whimper. "I have to...watch you touch me?"

I stroke her breasts. "Yes. I want you to see how beautiful you are. I want you to see how sexy you are. I want you to see my hands on you and know you are mine."

Her shy eyes lift to mine, watching me in the glass as she nestles against me. "Okay. I'll try."

"Don't try." I give her pussy another spank. "Obey."

Dipping my fingers inside her, I feel more slickness there than before. I lean down, nipping at her earlobe. "Your pussy gets so wet when I spank it. You love it when I spank you, don't you, you bad girl?"

She gives a little moan, her hips moving, the fullness of her ass cheeks rubbing against me. I push two fingers inside her, stretching her and filling her.

She's being a good girl, watching me in the reflection. My cock hardens at the look of shame that fills her gaze. "Oh, Preston…it's too…much. I can't watch."

"Yes, you can," I whisper as I stroke her. "Look how beautiful you look."

I lock my eyes on hers, holding her there while I touch her. I alternate circling her clit with fingering her, my eyes on her, my other hand cupping her breast and pinching at her nipple.

Her hips start to pick up a rhythm as they circle against me. She's panting, her skin dampening, her thighs trembling. I bring her just to the peak of climax and I stop.

"What? Wait!" she cries as I grab her hips.

Lifting her from my lap, I bend her over the edge of the bed. She can still see herself in the mirror, her torso stretched over the bedding, her feet planted on the floor. I pull down my jeans, freeing my cock while I watch her clutch the blankets with anticipation.

Grabbing her cheeks, I spread her thighs, nestling the head of my cock at her warm, wet entrance. It's too much for her, seeing me behind her, my hands smoothing over the naked skin of her back. Her head falls, her gaze dropping to the bed.

Sliding my hand over her curves, I spank her. Hard. "Eyes on the mirror," I say.

Making a shame-filled whimper, she rests her cheek on the bed, turning her face to the mirror. Grabbing her hips, I keep my eyes on her as I thrust forward, entering her fully with one hard shove.

Her mouth gapes, her eyes wide as she takes all of me at once. She's so tight, her body stretching around me, as I move inside her. She reaches back, grabbing at me, clutching my arm, wanting to hold onto something to anchor her.

Rolling my hips, I move back and forth, filling her then bringing it back. Smoothing my hands up her back, I grab handfuls of her hair. I pull her head back, slapping her ass as I fuck her. The mirror's forgotten. Her spine dips as she arches her back, her head coming toward me.

"Oh my God. Oh my God, Preston."

"Don't you mean, oh my devil?" I ask, slapping her ass again.

Her sex clenches around my cock, her muscles tighten as I pump inside her. The climax tightens in my balls, rising up and shooting through my stomach. I want to be closer to her. Giving a moan, I scoop her up, flipping her onto her back on the bed.

A smile spreads over her face as her thighs fall open for me. In one ragged breath, I'm back inside her, right where I need to be. I fuck her harder, faster, the lines of where her body ends and mine begins blend into one.

She curls around me, clinging to me, her fingers digging into my shoulders. She buries her face in the crook of my neck. I kiss her hair, her face, her shoulder. She gives a soft cry as she comes, clenching tighter and tighter around me as she comes.

She relaxes against me while I chase down my own pleasure. I come hard and fast, filling her with my seed. Marking her as mine. A crazy thought erupts in the pleasure of my orgasm. A temporary moment of insanity.

The thought of what if...

What if there was nothing inside her to stop us from having a baby?

Preston, get a grip. You're one lovesick puppy. I laugh at my craziness, gathering her in my arms, the warmth of afterglow relaxing me as I carry her to the shower.

"I can walk, you know," she giggles.

"I like carrying you," I say.

We shower under the warm water of my rain shower. I lather her skin, her hair, cleaning every inch of her body. Afterward, I towel her skin dry, kissing each one of her toes.

I dress in a dark suit. She gives me a hungry look of approval.

She finds the things Charlie has left for her. A matching satin bra and panty set, a little black cocktail dress with thin straps for sleeves, a case full of new makeup products, all perfectly matched to her skin tone.

I leave her to play. When she's done, she looks absolutely stunning. I don't tell her, but I think she's even prettier without a lick of makeup on.

We're the last to arrive at the rooftop bar. I figured I'd let her make a grand entrance. The night air is cool, but they've got the propane heaters and firepits roaring, letting off heat. White globe lights hang from overhead.

All heads turn to us. Pride swells in my chest, suddenly glad my night in got canceled. I'm happy to be showing her off, introducing her to everyone, and this gathering is the perfect place to do it. It's the first time I've ever brought a woman to a family event. Half the faces in the crowd are shocked that I've got a girl on my arm.

Rockland and Tess come over first.

"Who's that?" Jules whispers to me.

"Just the head of the family and his wife," I tease.

"What!" Her knees go weak, her fingers digging into my arm. She recovers quickly, offering a smile as they approach.

"Hello, Jules." Rockland leans down, brushing a kiss over her cheek. "We've heard so much about you."

Jules' brow crinkles as she shoots a glance at me. "Really?"

I hold in a groan. Rich always blames the women, but I know he's the one who's been spreading gossip about me and Jules.

"Yes." Tess laughs, the sound high and tinkling like bells. She tosses her red hair over her shoulder. "And let me tell you, you've made quite an impression on this young man. You're the *only* one we've heard anything about."

Jules takes Tess's hand, shaking it daintily. "Lovely to meet you," she says.

We spend the first half of the evening being passed from hug to handshake. They're just as smitten with her as I am. Finally, when they've all gotten their time in, I get Jules back in my arms.

We dance for the rest of the night. I take her back to my place, both of us heady from champagne. We have sex again, but this time it's slow and sweet and afterward a strange fear tears through me.

Having her here at my house, with my family, makes me realize that I don't want to go another day without her in my arms.

She falls asleep, naked, curled up under my left arm. I pull the covers over her, trying to finish a few emails on my phone with my free hand. I get a text. I saved Beau's number in my phone.

When the contact pops up, it makes me chuckle.

*Date Crashing Cowboy*

But when I see the picture he's sent through, my laughter dies in my throat.

It's a picture of me. The day of my eighteenth birthday. The day my life took a ninety-degree turn.

It's...the mugshot.

Beau:

*Does she know you're a criminal*

*With a record?*

"Get your facts straight, man. Criminal, yes. Record, no." The Bachmans wiped my slate clean the day I was initiated into the family. I'm surprised he even found this old pic. The family is thorough. He must have been digging deep, gotten into the sheriff's office for a paper file. I guess the Joneses have people too. "God, why is he digging up old shit on me?"

I stare at the picture. Because he loves Jules. I can't blame him for that. I respect that the man is looking out for her, but he needs to back off. She's mine.

I won't let him or anyone else get in the way of us.

I reply.

*Why does it matter*

Beau:

*It would matter to her*

He's absolutely right. But for all the wrong reasons. Why can't this damn kid just keep his nose in his own business? He has no idea what happened that night, or how it affected the trajectory of my life.

I throw out a string of messages.

*If you tell her it will hurt her*

*But not in the way you think*

*I understand you want to protect her*

*How are you protecting her if you hurt her*

Beau:

*I don't want to hurt her*

I think of how sad Jules was in the car, driving up to the city, how lost she looked. Her words echo through my mind.

*When you find out the past isn't what you thought it was...your whole world turns upside down.*

I want to kick his ass. Why couldn't he leave well enough alone?

I throw out a Hail Mary.

*Then don't tell her*

*At least not until you talk to me face to face*

*Deal?*

I'm relieved by his response.

*Deal*

I slip the phone into my inside jacket pocket and run my hand through my hair.

What a shitty way to end a perfect night.

## 15

# Jules

I hate to leave the Village, I hate to leave him, but the thought of my responsibilities at home tug at me and I'll go crazy if I leave this thing with my dad hanging out there too long.

My bag is packed, sitting on his hall table by the front door.

We're in his kitchen, hovering over cold cups of coffee. I don't want this time to end, but I've got to get going. "That was a beautiful night. Thank you for taking me. And thanks for coming to get me at the last minute. I wish I could stay longer, but I need to go home and sort this all out with my dad."

"There's no way I'm letting you go back there alone. Not after the state you were in last time you were there." He dumps our cups in the sink, washing them out.

I don't want to burden him. He's here because he needs to work. There's no reason to involve him in my crazy family drama. "I'll call Beau if I need someone," I say.

His eyes hold mine. "No. You won't."

Is he serious? His gaze is burning through mine, daring me to argue.

He's serious.

Boundaries, Jules. You have to set boundaries with men like the Bachmans.

I put on my best lecture voice. "I'd like to tell you two things I just heard that I didn't like. First, there is no you 'letting' me go home. If I want to go home, I will. And secondly, you can't tell me I can't see Beau. What is your problem with him, anyway?"

He runs a hand through his hair, leaving it standing on end. "Look. He and I have some business between us we need to settle. I don't want you talking to him until he and I have had a face-to-face. I'm going to set him straight."

What problems could they possibly have with one another, other than a few childish spars over our Scrabble game? "Set him straight? Preston, what's gotten into you? You two barely know one another."

Agitated, Preston paces the floor as he speaks. "Why is he so into you, anyway?"

"We're friends. We have been for a long time." I toss my hand on my hip. "Why, is that a problem?"

He scoffs. "I have female friends and I sure as hell don't keep as close of an eye on them as he does with you."

"But you look out for Richmond, don't you? What's the difference?" I ask.

"What's the difference?" He stares at me like I'm crazy. "Can't you see the man is in love with you?"

*No.*

*Noooooo...*

This is *not* happening.

I try to hold back but it bubbles up from my belly, tickling my throat. I can't stop it from coming. I let out a loud laugh but in trying to hide it, it turns into the most hideous snort.

"Are you," he stares me down, "snorting at me?"

I shake my head, covering my mouth with my hand. "Oh my gosh, Preston. You're jumping to the wrong conclusions. You don't have anything to worry about between me and Beau. I promise. We're just friends."

His voice is icy. "I know you're his friend, but he thinks of you as more than a friend. I can tell."

"Preston, Beau is not into me." I hate to out someone when it's not my place, but this is just ridiculous. "The man is gay."

His brows shoot up. "He is?"

"Yes. He told me a few years ago at my best friend's wedding. We sat next to one another, and I was feeling a little desperate and I started flirting with him and he put his hand on mine and said, 'Jules, let me stop you right there,' and then he told me." I remember that night fondly. That's really when our friendship took off.

"Why didn't you tell me earlier?" he asks.

"I don't exactly make it my business to announce my friends' sexuality when I introduce them." I put on a fake announcer's voice. "Preston Bachman, meet Beau Jones. He's a gorgeous blond-haired, blue-eyed cowboy, with meticulously gelled hair, suspiciously well-dressed for a rancher, and...gay."

He doesn't laugh at my joke. He's still upset about something. But what?

"Tell me what's going on," I say.

He locks eyes with me, taking that commanding tone that sometimes comes over him. "Promise me you won't talk to him before I do. It's important."

I'm torn. Beau's been in my life for years. Preston means the world to me. I don't want to choose between them.

My phone rings. *Saved by the bell.* A perfect distraction to break the ice and get out of making any promises I can't keep.

"Sorry. I've got to check this in case it's my dad." I step out into the back garden before Preston can reply. I pull the glass door shut behind me.

It's not my dad calling. It's Beau.

Why would he be calling? Is my dad okay? "Hey, what's up? Everything okay?"

I glance through the glass. Preston is watching me. Still pacing.

"Yes. I just checked on him. He's fine. I told him you'd be here later today."

I breathe a sigh of relief. "Oh, good. Thanks so much for stopping by."

"Yeah." There's a beat of silence and I'm about to ask if he's okay when Beau's voice comes back through the phone. "I was up all night, debating whether to tell you but it was making me sick, you not knowing, so I just picked up the phone and called you."

"What is going on?" I ask.

"Ask him if he's ever been arrested," he says.

"Huh? What are you talking about?" Beau's not making sense.

He slows his words. "Ask your new Bachman boyfriend if he's ever been arrested."

"Why?" I say.

"Because. When I found out that you were dating one of them—"

I stop him. "Don't say it like that, Beau."

"Fine," he says. "When I found out you were going out with a man who has ties to the mafia—"

"They're not a mafia." What are they? "They're just a tight-knit family who like their privacy."

"Jules..." He uses the *get real* tone he sometimes favors.

"Okay, okay. We all know where the Bachmans got their start but the *no alcohol on the premises* Joneses made their fortune bootlegging back in the day. Didn't they? I really don't care. I like Preston. A lot."

He says, "Preston was arrested here. One town over. That night he got in the car with you."

"What?" Time stops. Tendrils of icicles rope around my spine. "You're sure?"

"Yes. I'm sure." Beau takes a deep breath. "What happened that night, Jules?"

Flashes of that night pop up in my mind. The water pooling around me, the darkness tugging at me. My lungs burning. My heart racing. The thrill of being young and alive. The warmth of his arms. Fiery kisses in the back seat of my car.

"Nothing, Beau. We drove around awhile. We made out. I used the key you gave me to unlock the side gate, the one up by the pond. I turned off my headlights and rolled it home at two miles per hour."

"And you dropped him off at home?" he asks.

I think back. "No. He wanted me to leave him at the gate. Said he wanted to take a walk. I left the gate unlocked for him." I never locked it back up. Nobody uses that gate; it could still be unlocked. I make a mental note to check when I get home.

"That's strange, don't you think? He just takes off walking away from town at who knows what time?" he asks.

What Beau is saying makes sense. It is strange. Especially if Preston really was arrested that same night. "I'll ask him, okay?"

"Thanks."

"Look. I need to come home. Preston's supposed to be working here with his friend Richmond. I already feel bad he had to come get me yesterday. Do you mind coming to get me? I know you like Daughtry's Clothing. I could meet you there."

He gives a sigh like he's put out, but I know he's not. He loves an excuse to come to the city. "I do have a Montana trip coming up and nothing to wear. See you at noon?"

"Thanks."

I've got a body in my closet and my mom might be a murderer and my dad is going crazy with guilt or whatever he's feeling, and now this. I promised Beau I'd get to the bottom of Preston's arrest, but I don't really want to ask him. Preston would have told me if he wanted me to know about it.

But Beau's planted the seed in my mind and now I'm wondering what happened after I dropped Preston off at the gate.

Preston is waiting in the kitchen, hands on his hips like a dad waiting for a daughter who's broken curfew.

"Hey," I say.

"Hey. How's your dad?"

"That wasn't my dad. That was Beau," I say.

The color drains from Preston's face. He has a visceral reaction, his hands slipping into his pockets, his eyes leaving mine. His voice dips down a full octave. "What did he want?"

Beau's right. Something's up. Why else would Preston be acting like this?

"Why were you arrested that night?" I ask.

He won't look at me. "I can't tell you."

"Why?"

Finally he drags his gaze up to meet mine. Anger burns in the blue-green pools of his irises. "I can't. Tell you."

He's scaring me. I've not seen him angry before. Why won't he just tell me what happened?

"I don't care that you've been arrested. I just hate that you don't trust me enough to tell me why," I say. "We were together that night. What happened after I left you at the gate?"

"Jules. Listen to me when I say I can't tell you." His gaze narrows. "You need to respect my request."

I can't. We're in too deep. "So I'm your girl when you want to sleep with me but when it comes to talking about your past…hell, our past. I was with you that night, for goodness' sake. Just tell me, Preston. How bad can it be…"

I let my words trail off, waiting for him to fill the empty space with the truth.

He doesn't.

Suddenly I'm very much the small-town good girl, out of place in this fancy Village with this handsome man full of dark secrets. Ones he won't trust me with. I'm still spinning out of control over my conversation with my dad.

Why all these secrets?

Now that this gaping canyon sits between the two of us, I just want to go home. I need to be there, with my dad, sorting out our own messy past.

And I'd rather do it alone.

"I think we need some time apart. I'm going home. And you hate it so much there anyway, I'd rather you didn't come with me."

"I don't hate it," he says.

"You've made it pretty clear."

"If you don't want me to stay with you, fine. But I'm driving you. You can be mad at me, you don't have to talk to me, hell, you don't even have to look at me, but I'm taking you back. Understand?" He gives me that *don't even argue* look of his.

"No, thank you." I brush past him, grabbing my bag from the hall table.

He grabs my arm. "Jules, you're being unreasonable."

"Am I?" I plead with him with my gaze.

Tell me, Preston, just tell me. But he denies me again, offering me nothing but silence.

"I already asked Beau to come get me. He's on the way." I tug away from his grasp.

"You are not walking out that door." His stare is all heat, daring me to move.

I can't let him tell me what to do. Not right now. "Preston. I really like you. But if you follow me out of here, you won't see me again. Give me the space I'm asking for. Please."

"You're giving me an ultimatum?" He looks like he wants to throw me over his shoulder and lock me up in a tower. "You sure you want to do that?"

He has to let me go. Or risk losing me forever. Hell—if he can't tell me about that night...he might have already. "Not an ultimatum. Just...I don't know. I'm leaving."

"You're just going to leave?" That warning brow just keeps going higher. "Because that's not the way to handle things between us. I'd like to know that things between us are resolved before we leave one another. You know, there are consequences in life when you leave things unresolved."

The word *consequences* makes my skin flush and my ass clench. Surely he doesn't mean those kinds of consequences, does he? I'm angry and I just need some space.

I force myself to meet his challenging gaze. "I'm leaving."

"I'll have someone let you out of the gates." He brushes a kiss against my cheek. His lips feel cool against my flushed skin.

"Goodbye."

"Take care," he says.

When he closes the door behind me, it feels like our final goodbye.

And he just lets me go.

## 16

Jules

I know I threatened him if he followed me, but somehow the idea that he's letting me walk down these stairs by myself and leave the Village without him by my side, it's too much. And suddenly, I'm doing that thing that I absolutely loathe when other girls do it.

Tell the man one thing and expect him to read your mind and know that you want him to do the opposite.

That isn't fair to anyone.

Get over it, Jules. You told him not to come. He's respecting your wishes. You should be happy about it.

I walk alone down the perfectly manicured sidewalks, walking by the perfectly gorgeous homes, passing the perfectly happy, successful, beautiful people. Leaving behind my *almost* perfect boyfriend.

Why won't he just tell me what happened? Why doesn't he trust me?

It sucks because I don't want to walk away from him right now. I want to resolve this yucky feeling between us. I really care about him—heck, I think I'm falling in love with the man. Am I being unreasonable? I don't know. I just know that it broke my heart when he wouldn't confide in me.

Honestly? I don't even really want to know if he doesn't want to tell me. I don't care what he did ten years ago. I'm so head over heels for who he is now.

I reach the gate. A massive man with a shaved head and a thick accent greets me. I don't remember him from the party last night. "Miss Verduce. Pleasure to meet you. I'm Ace. Preston asked me to escort you past the gates."

"Thank you."

He waves his watch by the black box in the wall. The first gate opens. My heart sinks a little as we walk through the stone corridor to the second black gate. *Goodbye, beautiful village.* He opens the second one and I step out onto the busy city sidewalk, alone.

*Goodbye, Preston.*

"Thank you, Ace." I offer him a wave.

He's got a smile on his face like he's laughing at an inside joke. "See you, Miss Verduce."

Are they all laughing at me? Word travels fast in their family. Do they know I've left behind the only man I've ever…I'm being paranoid. No one is thinking of me. I heave a sigh. I've got at least an hour before Beau will be here to meet me.

Glancing up at the signs, I try to decide which store to waste time in. Ace catches my eye. He's still standing at the gate, that smile on his face. He's staring out at the street. I turn, my gaze following the line of his.

Parked at the curb is a gorgeous black BMW SUV, with an even more gorgeous man leaning against it. Preston's got his arms crossed over his chest. His brows are raised, that stern look on his face that makes my belly flip-flop.

He's looking right at me. His stare sends pulses through me. Lifting a hand, he crooks his finger at me, beckoning.

I go to him, skipping all the fake drama, the *why'd you follow me, I told you not to follow me, blah, blah, blah* crap.

"Hey," I say.

"Hey." He holds out his hand for my bag.

Obediently, I hand it to him.

"Did you really think I'd let you go off on your own like that?"

I give a shrug. "I don't know. I was surprised."

"Well, I couldn't let you just leave town like that. I was just giving you a minute to cool off and collect your thoughts." He walks around the car, putting my bag in the trunk, all while somehow managing to keep his heavy gaze locked on my face.

By the time he comes back to me, I'm full of heat.

Slipping a hand up the back of my hair, he discreetly gathers a knot of it, holding me in place. He brushes his lips over my cheeks, his mouth finding my ear. "I'll take you home. But first we need to have a little chat."

The words *little chat* make me shiver. "Okay. But are you going to at least say something about what we were fighting about when I left your house first?"

"I will. When I can. Can you accept that?"

Can I? He stares into my eyes and I can't give him any other answer than, "Yes."

"I texted Beau. Explained to him that you will no longer be needing a ride. That I've got you covered."

He says *got you covered* like he has plans for me. Ones I might not be ready for.

Heat pricks at my skin and my throat feels tight. "Um…okay. Sounds…good?"

"We have something between us we need to discuss."

He opens my door for me, giving me that *you're in so much trouble* look I'm starting to love. What the heck has come over me? What's changed me from being an independent woman to a melting puddle of love?

*He has.*

Submissively, I slip into the leather seat. He pulls the buckle over my lap, leaving me with a chaste kiss. My thighs press together. I don't know what he has in store for me, but my body feels electrified with anticipation over it.

We drive in silence, static energy buzzing between us. His fingers stroke my thighs and the light touch makes me wetter and wetter. By the time he pulls up to our stop, I'm squirming in my seat.

He parks the car in front of what looks like a dive bar. There's an unmarked black door next to its entrance.

"Where are we going?" I ask.

He points to the black door. "In there."

I don't ask any more questions. He comes and gets me, grabs my hand, and leads me to the door. People pass by, staring at their phones or thinking of where they're headed, paying no attention to us as we slip inside.

"What is this place?" I ask.

He tugs me down a long hall to a room that holds nothing but a black leather Chesterfield sofa, its arms low and round. "Just a place where we do business sometimes. It's a nice, quiet place to talk. Don't you think?"

The door closes with a click.

"I've been thinking it over and, well," his tongue runs over his lips, "now that you're my girl, I think you need to know how things are going to be between us. I need to show you."

What is he talking about? Who is this man and what has he done with my Preston? A thrill flips my belly over and my panties become increasingly damp. "I don't know what you're talking about."

He slips a hand up the side of my face, cupping my cheek. "When I made you my girl, when I fucked you and claimed you for my own, it was with the intention of making you my wife one day."

"Your...wife?"

"And if you're going to be my wife, you need to know how a Bachman marriage operates. And that little trick you pulled at my place? Trying to run from me, instead of figuring things out with me? That," his hands travel over the curves of my ass, clutching it in his fingers, "is not allowed."

*Holy. Cow.*

I've never been more wet or more scared in my life. What does he plan on doing to me? Is he going to...punish me?

Other than the few smacks he laid on my ass at my place, I've never been spanked. The feel of his hand against my bare skin, it stung but in the most delicious way. What would it feel like to have him do it again?

My breath comes heavy as he kisses me. It's a hard, possessive, punishing kiss and it makes my heart stop in my chest. My knees go weak. I lean further back onto the arm of the couch for support.

*If I'm his girl...and I am, I so am his girl...*

I guess that means he can do anything he wants with me. Anything at all.

Fear and excitement course through my body with such ferocity I can't separate one emotion from the other. My body is on high alert, responding to his every touch.

My nipples grow harder, his hands grabbing my breasts with rough caresses. My sex is empty and throbbing from wanting his touch so very badly. He breaks our kiss, cupping my flushed face between his hands.

"Are you my girl?" he asks. "Are you giving me the gift of your submission?"

My answer is only a whisper but I'm so sure of it, I feel like I'm shouting it from the top of the Bachman's rooftop bar. "Yes. I am."

"There are consequences when you leave things unresolved." There's that little word again. Only now, it seems like a big, fat, scary word. "Take off those jeans. Now."

With fumbling, shaking fingers, I obey.

Under his heavy gaze, shame fills me as I shimmy them over my hips and off my body. My pink panties have hearts on them. Geez—did I really grab this pair to spend the night at his house? They seem so childish now.

But there's nothing childish about what's going through my body and my mind. He reaches for them, stroking a finger over the seam of my sex, the tip of his finger hovering over a heart that just happens to be centered over my clit.

He circles it with the lightest pressure. "Cute."

Brushing past me, he sends chill bumps over my flesh. He takes a seat in the center of the sofa, staring up at me. His long arms rest along the back of the couch. Spreading his legs wide, he calls for me.

"Come lay yourself over my lap, baby."

I can't. This is wrong. *So* fucking wrong. But I want it so badly.

Inching my way to him, I summon the courage to do as he asks. I stare down at his muscular thighs spread over the leather cushions. How do I do this gracefully?

You just do it.

I crawl across his lap, resting my upper body on the couch, my elbows sinking into the soft cushion. My legs sprawl out behind me, the backs of my feet resting on the arm of the sofa.

"Good girl." He grabs my hips, lifting me and centering my ass over the middle of his thigh.

My face burns with shame, I want to bury it in my hands. My knees tremble and my pussy aches. I'm so wet I want to squirm, press my thighs together, do something to get some friction, some pressure down there.

His hand lands on my ass. I let out a yelp. "Ow!" The fire spreads over my skin, pulling me from my hurricane of thoughts.

Stroking his hand over his spank, he speaks in a low tone. I can feel his words rumble in my core. "You don't run from me. You never run from me." His hand comes down again, a stinging smack over my panty-covered curves. The loud sound echoes through the empty room, followed by my wail.

It hurts, oh it hurts, but somehow the pain is pleasure and I feel the sting travel from my ass to the apex of my thighs. His fingers part my thighs, creeping between my legs. Brushing over the gusset of my panties, he gives a dark chuckle.

"So wet for me. You like it when I spank you, don't you? You like knowing I'm in control. That I'll always take care of you." His hand comes down again, right over the center of my ass. "And that I'll punish you when you're bad."

His fingers go back to my panties, patting me through the damp fabric.

I need to come.

"Please." The whine rises in my voice, with need surging in my core. "Please make me come."

"You will."

*Thank goodness...*

His hand cups my ass cheek. "I have to punish you first."

He arranges me with my forearms resting on the low, wide arm of the sofa, my torso tilted up. He slides an arm around me, his hand flattening against my clavicle.

He wraps his fingers lightly around my neck.

Possessive, controlling. His fingertips stroke my skin. The feeling is so...intense, so erotic, I lose my breath.

My ass is still centered directly over his lap, my knees sinking in the buttery leather.

I feel his fingers capture the elastic waistband at the back of my panties. Noooo.... I let out a low moan. To be over his lap like this, it's overwhelming. To have him pull my panties down, baring me in this strange, empty room?

Giving them a little tug, he slowly inches them down a bit. He's going to take his time pulling them down. I can tell. He's going to prolong my humiliation as long as possible.

The leather is cool against the bare skin of my legs, but my face is on fire. The white heat of shame licks at my cheeks.

He dips his hand under my panties, squeezing my right ass cheek with his palm as the fingertips of his other hand stroke my jawline. "Have you been bad?"

"Yes."

"Let's get these panties down." He rolls them down slowly, leaving them tucked up under the very bottom curve of my ass. The cool air rushes over my heated flesh.

"Never walk away from me again." A sharp spank lands, making me suck in air between my teeth. "We do these things together." His hand lands in a volley of short, stinging smacks. My ass jiggles under his palm.

The sting settles into my flesh. I wriggle my hips like it will alleviate the fire he's set on my ass. Sucking air between my teeth, I whisper, "I understand."

"You look so beautiful laying over my lap, just like I knew you would."

He's fantasized about this? He's imagined spanking me? I like the idea of him thinking dirty thoughts about me when I'm not around.

The tip of his finger dips beneath the elastic band around my cheek. He pulls it back, letting it snap against the top of my thigh. "Have you been wanting a man to take control?"

"I don't know…I've never done this before…"

He runs a finger down the bare cleft of my ass. I hold in a groan.

"No." He pushes past my cheeks. Where is his finger going? I wriggle my hips over his lap, trying to get away from his touch. "What are you doing?"

His finger inches closer. He is *soooo* going there. I wriggle harder, but his fingers tighten around my neck, making me pause.

"I'll never forget the day I made you mine. And one day, I'll claim you here too." A whine of disagreement rises in the back of my throat as he pushes against my tight entrance.

"Um…I don't think we'll be doing that."

"I know we will." He leans over me, catching my eye. "Now, if you want to come, beg me for it."

"Please, Preston, make me come. Please!" I wiggle my hips emphatically, dying without his touch. Finally his hands return to me. Stroking me, making me buck hard against his thighs. The climax rolls through me, my hands clutching at the leather cushions.

How did I go so long without him? Without this?

And what happens to *us* when his time in Cedar Creek ends?

## 17

# Preston

Mr. Verduce folds his hands together, flattens his palms to the kitchen table, then folds them again. He still wears his wedding ring, a gold band circling the ring finger of his left hand.

He slips his glasses from the bridge of his nose to the top of his head, heaving a sigh. His shoulders curl in, the weight of the world pressing down on them.

"I'm sorry about the other day, Julie Belle. That migraine came out of nowhere." He rubs his forehead between his thumb and forefinger. "At least that means that this whole illness has been psychological. Hopefully after today, after telling you everything…I'll be on the road to recovery."

Jules reaches out, patting her dad's arm. "Whatever it is, Dad, it'll be better to have it out in the open, rather than buried on the inside."

He catches her eye. "I don't know about that. It's pretty heavy stuff I'm about to tell you."

"I can handle it. I just want to know," she pleads.

Mr. Verduce turns to me. "I owe you a serious apology, son. I'm very sorry for how I treated you in the past." His gaze holds mine a beat longer than necessary.

I give him a nod. "Water under the bridge," I say.

"Thank you. And thank you for being here, Preston." I think it's the first time he's used my real name. "Nice car, by the way."

"Oh, the Ghost? Jules deserves it. She's taking care of everyone. Why not do it in a nice car?"

Jules' cheeks go pink but she doesn't protest.

"So true, young man." He gives a half smile, the most he can muster in this situation. "I appreciate the support you are giving Jules. I'm glad you were here for her when I wasn't."

"It's my pleasure." I run my hand over Jules' back. She shoots me a grateful look. I love being here for her, being her protector.

We were both surprised when we showed up at her house and her dad welcomed me in his arms with a hug. I guess having your own dark past absolves you from judging others for theirs. I'm glad we've moved on.

"Okay. Where to start?" He stares up at the ceiling.

My lawyer brain tells me I need to step in or we're not going to get anywhere. "Let's start with Jules' mom. Do you know where she went when she left? Have you heard from her at all?"

"She...did something." The color drains from his face. He starts to stammer, his hand going to his chest. "I...she...she asked me to h-hide it. To hide what she did."

Jules' words are a haunted whisper. "What did she do?"

He buries his head in his hands.

*This is bad.*

"Mr. Verduce. Can you tell us what she did?" I ask.

"I can't do it." A shuddering breath tears through him. "I can't."

Jules shoots me a desperate look. "What do we do?" she whispers.

I look from her to her crumbling father. I don't think he can handle this. I'm worried about his health. His face is pale, almost green. He's clutched at his chest more than once during this conversation.

"Let's take a break," I say, pushing my chair back from the table and standing. "Jules. Can I see you outside for a second?"

She follows me out.

Leaving the front door open, I stand where I can see her father. "Baby, I'm worried about your dad. I think he's not well."

She shuffles the tip of her sneaker against the pavement, staring at the ground. "He said it's psychological. That he'll get better when he tells me."

"I understand that. But he's showing signs of—"

I'm watching him squeeze his eyes shut tight like he's in pain. He leans heavily against the card table. He's grabbing his left arm.

*Shit.* I make my voice calm. "Call an ambulance, Jules. I think your dad is having a heart attack."

"What?" Her head snaps up, her eyes wide. She looks over her shoulder. "Oh! Dad!"

We run to the kitchen. Jules is calling for help. I'm wrapping my arms around him, holding him in his chair so he doesn't collapse to the floor.

An hour later, they're preparing him for surgery. He's got a blocked artery in his heart. He's having a coronary angioplasty. They're going to open the clogged artery with a tiny balloon, widening the blocked vessel to let blood flow to the heart. Apparently, the EKG he had when he was first trying to find out what was causing his dizzy spells can't detect a clog. He would have needed a nuclear stress test, cardiac pet scan, coronary CT angiogram or traditional coronary angiogram.

None of which were ordered for him by his physicians. Then he decided to take a more homeopathic route, going on the retreat. Meantime his problem was getting worse.

Mr. Verduce's going to be in surgery for three to five hours. Up at the front desk of the hospital I get in a floor manager's ear and promise a cash donation to the kids' wing, basically pulling a Bachman card, so we're given a private hospital room to wait in.

Jules is a wreck. She sits beside me, rocking back and forth in her chair. "Come here," I say, gathering her in my arms. I pull her onto my lap and hold her. I just let her cry.

She wipes at her tears. "I had no idea, Preston. How did I miss that? I mean, you were there all of what? Five minutes? And you diagnosed him right away."

I shake my head. "He grabbed his left arm. That's the only way I knew. You couldn't have known." I stroke her hair away from her face and kiss the tears from her cheeks.

Beau comes into the room. His eyes meet mine but instead of malice there's an almost apologetic look there. Does he feel bad about breaking his word to me, to not talk to Jules before I did?

I sure as hell hope so. This thing with her dad is at the forefront of her mind but when he's in recovery, she's still going to want to know why I was arrested.

Thanks a lot, cowboy.

"Hey, man." Beau takes a seat next to Jules' empty one. "Hey, Jules."

She slips off my lap, going back to her chair and hugging him. "Oh, Beau. You should have seen him. His face was all gray and..." She chokes back a sob.

He squeezes her tight, then lets her go. Beau's eyes meet mine over the top of her head. "We're lucky Preston knew what to do. He's a good guy." He gives me a nod.

That was an apology if I ever heard one.

Jules seems calmer in Beau's presence, so I let him stay, letting our little misunderstanding pass. He was just looking out for her and if he's important to her, I'll get used to him.

Besides, we can talk about cars.

"What was he doing? When he had the heart attack?" Beau asks.

"Oh, Beau. You don't even know about that part yet." Jules heaves a sigh, looking to me to tell the story.

"Jules found this package in her hall closet a few nights ago. Something big and heavy and strange. Her father had done some demo work and the—thing, we still don't know what it is—was hidden in the wall between the hall closet and Jules' bedroom."

Beau lets out a low groan. "Oh God. This is all my fault." He goes white.

A strange silence fills the room. "What do you mean?" Jules asks.

He shakes his head. "I don't know how I could have handled the situation any differently, but if he had a damn heart attack over it, I fucked up."

"He had the heart attack because of his cholesterol. Not because of anything you did," I say.

"What happened, Beau?" Jules tugs at his arm. "Please. Tell me quickly. I don't think I can take any more secrets."

Beau takes a deep breath. "You know when my family moved to Montana?"

"Yes," she says.

Beau speaks quickly, as if wanting the story out in the world as fast as possible. "Well, before we left, my brother was doing some work under your dad's house. You were still in the city at the time. He was replacing some rotten floorboards that ran along the front of the house. While he was under there, taking down the bad boards, part of that package just about fell on him."

Jules nods. "A body. It *is* a body, isn't it? My mom killed someone, and my dad hid it for her?"

"No, Jules. That's not what happened," he says.

Her hand flutters over her chest, a deep exhale leaving her body. "Thank goodness! What was it?"

Apparently, his brother went home and got Beau. They confronted the reverend. With a tightness in his voice and a heaviness in his shoulders, Beau tells us the rest of the story, what Jules' dad told him and his brother that day, finally putting the mystery to bed.

*Jules' mom was unstable. Her manic episodes were getting worse. I took her to the doctor. They put her on these antidepressants. They worked at first. I had some hope. Then, they stopped working. She became more...upset. I didn't know what to do.*

*Years later, I did some investigating and I believe she was misdiagnosed. The manic episodes, followed by the depressive moods, I think she was bipolar. I found out depression medication alone can be dangerous for that disorder, but I didn't know that then.*

*I found her, lying in bed, wearing her favorite dress. A vase of freshly picked wildflowers was on the night table beside her.*

*Along with a note...and the empty pill bottles.*

*In the note, she told me she couldn't take this life anymore. That she was sorry, but she had to go. She told me that her one wish was that Jules never, ever know what happened to her. She wanted her daughter's memories of her to be of the fun things they did together. She liked the idea of Jules thinking she was off in the world somewhere, doing big things.*

*So, I gave her her wish.*

*I told no one. In the middle of the night, I buried her in the town graveyard. I marked her grave with a stone.*

Beau ends with, "He couldn't finish the story."

Her mother was...gone? And her father never told her the truth?

Jules just sits there in silence. Is she in shock? Should I get a doctor? There's plenty of them.

Finally she whispers, "She's...dead?"

"I'm sorry you had to find out this way," Beau said. "I wanted your dad to be the one to tell you."

"She's really dead," Jules says, more to herself than to us. "I just...I mean I thought she was sailing in Europe or hiking the Appalachian Trail when I pictured her. I never once thought she was...gone."

"You okay?" I ask her. It's a stupid thing to ask, of course she's not. How can she be? But damn, this woman is so strong. Somehow, she manages to hold it together.

"Yes. I'm fine. Just a little shaken is all." She turns to Beau. "I'm sorry you had to deal with that. What happened next?"

Beau takes a deep breath. I don't think this cowboy is used to talking this much at once. He says, "After hours of debate, my brother and I decided to let it go, figuring it was the reverend's personal business and in the past. But then, Jules, you moved home. It was killing me that you didn't know..." His words trail off.

"That my mom was dead?" she asks with a dark laugh.

"Yeah. That," he says. "I told him he had to tell you the truth. I'm sorry I didn't make him do it sooner."

"It's okay," Jules says.

"I'd forgotten all about it until a few months ago when you mentioned something about your mom and how you thought she was probably enjoying the fall weather wherever she was." Beau runs a hand over the back of his neck, clearly feeling guilty. "In that moment, I realized he hadn't told you. I went straight to your dad that day and told him, either he tells you or I would. Mr. Verduce kept begging for more time. But finally, last week, I told him that his time was up. That's when the reverend started demo-ing the closet."

"What is that—thing?" she asks.

"Your dad said he couldn't bear to get rid of your mother's things, but he couldn't have them around, either. He wrapped them up in a tarp, hid them in the wall. I guess he wanted to have her stuff out for you when he told you the truth. Maybe it would soften the blow? To have some of her things?"

"That makes sense," she says. "I'm just so relieved that it's not a body..."

"Sorry, Jules. If I'd have known you found it and were thinking those things, I would have told you myself." Beau looks sick.

We sit in silence, letting her process the whole thing. Finally, she speaks.

She says, "All these years I thought she left. I thought she left...*me*. I couldn't help but to feel, deep down, that it wasn't only Cedar Creek that wasn't enough for her. I thought maybe *I* wasn't enough. It's even sadder to hear that she ended her life...that she's not out there somewhere, living her best life. That's just...so sad." Tears glisten in her gaze.

"That is sad," I say. Beau agrees.

"And it's sad that she suffered so badly. That she couldn't get the help she needed." She shakes her head. "And my poor dad? To have to do that for your wife? To have to hide a secret like that? I don't know how he did it."

The three of us spend the next few hours while Jules' dad is in surgery talking about what happened. It seems healthy for Jules, the weight visibly lifting from her countenance as we speak.

A nurse pops in to tell us the surgery is going well. We sit and hang out, the atmosphere in the room growing lighter. My arms never leave Jules.

The doctor comes in, tired but triumphant. "Hey, folks. Everything went great."

He fills us in on the recovery her dad will face. Jules will need to stay with him, to nurse him back to health. Looks like I'll be working remotely. I'm not leaving her side.

When her dad is ready for a visit, we go to his room. "Julie Belle, I owe you an explanation." He reaches for her hand.

She takes his hand in hers, slipping into the seat beside his bed. "Dad, Beau told me everything. We can talk about it another time. I'm fine. I promise. Just rest."

"Oh, that's good, Jules. That's really nice..." Relief washes over his face. Another pump of meds from the IV must flow through him because he's nodding off to sleep.

The nurse tells us visiting hours are over. Jules gives her dad a kiss. "Bye, Dad. See you tomorrow."

The three of us walk out of the hospital together. Beau and I shake hands. I get Jules situated in the car, and then I realize—I don't know where I'm taking her. It seems like a lot to go back to her house tonight.

I pat her thigh. "You know what? I've got a half a pan of Charlie Bachman's lasagna in my freezer and it's the best I've ever had. Do you like pasta?"

"My grandmother was born in Italy. Of course I love pasta," she laughs.

"I think this is a great night for comfort food. What do you say we go back to mine? I can have you back here as early as you want tomorrow morning."

She gives me a grateful look. "That sounds nice. Thanks."

"And I know we need to talk about the arrest, but I don't think this is the time. Let's put that aside for a few days and focus on your dad. Agreed?"

"Agreed." She rests her head on my shoulder and it's the best feeling in the world. She gives a small sigh. Her head pops back up. "Actually, I have something I want to say about that."

"Okay..." I just want her head back on my shoulder. "Tell me."

"Going through this whole thing with you by my side, it made me realize I was wrong. I owe you an apology."

"Why would you owe me an apology?" I ask.

"I was wrong. I thought that you not telling me about your arrest that night was a case of you not trusting me enough to tell me. But you obviously have my best interests at heart. You take care of me, you put me first. So, if there's something you don't want me to know about that night, I realize you're not telling me because you're protecting me from something." She shoots me a look. "I wish I would have respected your wishes."

"Baby. You blow me away. You're so strong, and you're always putting others first. Please don't apologize."

"I just want you to know that I trust you. And no, I don't want to talk about the arrest in a few days. I don't want to talk about it...ever."

I accept her decision.

She's hurting so much already...

I don't want to hurt her again.

# 18

# Jules

*Six Months Later...*

I'm sixteen, flying down a dirt road in my convertible, Preston, the handsome baseball player that all the girls want...sitting in my passenger seat. Why did he flag me down? I didn't even know he knew I existed.

I mean, we all *know* one another, it's a small town, but he hasn't been here long and everyone is obsessed with him. There's just this buzz around him. He's hot and fun and...hot.

The car jolts as I hit a bump, the impact pulling me from my thoughts. "Shoot! What was that?" Did I hit something?

"Dunno." Preston turns and looks over his shoulder. "Slow up. Let me get out and see."

I pull the car over and he hops out, jogging back to where we hit the bump. He comes back. "Just the end of a branch sticking out over the road. And your tire looks fine. Nothing to worry about."

"Good."

He gets back in the car. "Hey, pull over here. I know a place." He points to a side road coming up on my left. One that leads to the river. We abandon my convertible on the side of the road. He gives me a wicked smile, tearing his shirt up over his head.

"Now you," he says.

I can't believe I'm doing it, but now I'm peeling my clothes off too, careful to keep my arms covering up as much as I can. Laughing, we leave our clothes on the bank of the river. I shy away from looking at his body, moving down to the river's edge.

The moonlight illuminates the night, casting a bluish tint over me. Wanting to hide my nakedness from him, I'm the first to jump in the water. It splashes around me, warming my skin against the cool night air.

*My first time skinny dipping...*

Laughing I burst up from the water, my arms crossed over my breasts. My feet dance against the smooth river stones. The water tugs at me, pulling at my hips. I hold my feet firm to the river bottom, splashing water at Preston.

"Come in deeper," I say. He seems further from me than he was just a moment ago. "Are you coming?"

"Careful of the current, Jules. Swim toward me."

The smile on my face is stretching up my cheeks. I feel so free.

"Now, Jules!" His brow knits together. "Come closer."

The tone in his voice makes me take a pause.

The current had been just a tug at my hips, but now it's a pull, a force to be reckoned with. He's so far from me. I need to get back to him. Dragging my arms through the water, I thrash my legs, trying to move to him.

"Jules? You okay?" He's swimming toward me.

I'm not making any progress. My feet search for the stones beneath me. I'm drifting, moving away from him, the space between us growing faster than I can comprehend. The invisible force drags me further and I fight back, trying to close the space between me and him.

But I can't.

Fear fills me. I'm sure I'll be lost, washed away by the strong water, pulled under or into the tangled roots growing along the side of the riverbank.

"Preston!" I dip below the surface, water threatening to fill my lungs.

The water rushes me further down the river. I'm bobbing up and down, gasping for breaths whenever I rise above the surface. Fear takes over, making my muscles tense, my body frantic.

I'm losing the fight.

I'm going under.

Strong arms wrap around me, embracing me, pulling me to the surface. Air fills my lungs, burning as they expand. I grab onto his strong shoulders, not wanting to go under again.

"I've got. You. I've got. You. Hold on tight. I won't let you go."

I cling to him.

"You saved me," I say, burying my face into the curve of his neck. "You saved me."

I wake, gasping for breath, my body curled in a ball. I feel the heat of him against me, his strong arms reaching out for me.

"It's okay, baby, I've got you," he says, pulling me close.

I'm in my room, with the familiarity of my bed, his warm comforting scent, the safety of his arms. We're in my bed, I know that now, but the dream was so real, my memories surfaced so vividly, it was as if I was reliving the moment exactly how it happened.

Preston brushes the hair back from my face, kissing the top of my head. He has no idea what woke me. His voice is thick with sleep. "Go back to sleep, birthday girl. Go back to sleep."

As I curl up against him, a deep relief settles over me. That night, that moment bonded us. I finally told my dad what happened, about the skinny-dipping and how Preston saved my life.

Dad thanked Preston for saving my life. Preston said it was his fault. That he never should have suggested swimming, putting me in harm's way in the first place. He promised my dad that as long as he lives, my safety, well-being, and happiness will be his first priority.

And all was well. And now, I'm warm and safe and dry and in his arms.

Today is my birthday. Twenty-six candles on my cake and I'm not a virgin. And I'm in love.

When I think of Preston, my heart wells, my body heats and I feel…happy.

So. Fucking. Happy.

His breaths return to the deep steady rhythm of sleep. I stir, wide awake.

Immediately following my father's return home, we had a beautiful service for my mom. Preston, Beau, Erin, and my dad and I were the only ones present. We didn't want any salacious gossip, just the final peaceful putting to rest of my mom's body.

Mom went through so much turmoil in her short life. I love looking out over the rose bushes and lilacs we planted over her grave, knowing she's resting beneath them.

Preston made me see a therapist three times a week for several weeks to process what I'd been through. At first, I tried to argue with him, but his stern ways and firm hand changed my mind, and he was right. It was healthy to unpack the crazy facts that I'd thought my mom left when actually she'd died, and that I thought I had a body hidden in my house.

Together, we opened the package of my mom's belongings. Her brightly colored clothing brought back so many memories of fun, crazy outings and last minute thrown-together parties. There was the small globe that we would sit together and spin. She'd put her finger on a random spot and tell me the name of the country and the things we would do when we would travel there one day.

The globe is what I thought was the head...

It's been...a lot. But Preston tells me I'm strong and I've only grown stronger.

He's told me to expect a surprise tonight. To wear my favorite dress. He's bought me dozens of beautiful dresses, but of course, I've chosen the green Versace.

I have no idea what he has planned, but I'm sure it will go down in Cedar Creek history.

We've been in town for six months, Preston working from his makeshift office in my bedroom while I play nurse to my father. I thought it was going to be a long, awkward road but instead we've become a cohesive family.

I know this can't last forever but my heart is torn between my commitment to my father and my future with Preston. My dad is almost ready for total independence; his "friend" Erin comes over almost every night. It's getting to be time for me to leave.

And where will I go? I know my dad and Erin are getting closer, moving faster than Preston and me. They want to start their own life together.

Which displaces me.

Preston has no desire whatsoever to stay at his dad's old house and I don't blame him. Eventually, he needs to get back to work in person. He wants me to move to the Village.

Without a ring on my finger I feel uncomfortable moving onto Bachman turf. They're all about commitment, family, and I'm not family. I'm trying to be patient. I know Preston's been a playboy for the last decade we've been apart. I don't expect him to change overnight for me.

Hell—I waited twenty-five years to lose my virginity, I can wait five more for a diamond.

*Am I right?*

He's sleeping so peacefully beside me; I just lie there, awake, lost in my thoughts, not wanting to wake him.

I try to guess what he's planned for my birthday tonight. Probably a sexy night in the city. My dad's healthy enough for us to leave town for the night and Erin's close by if he needs anything. Heck, the truth is my dad will probably be delighted to have a night with me and Preston out of the house.

The past six months I've been wearing sweats and a tee, taking care of my father's needs twenty-four seven. If I'm not caring for him, then I'm running errands for his elderly parishioners.

It's really how I knew Preston was the one. He never wavered during all the un-sexy sleeping in my room across from my dad who's snoring like a boar, me wearing that old sports bra and washed out panties and yet—the fire between us never dulled.

There's been some serious sneaking around. We've had sex in just about every private place we can find in this town, not to mention a few overnights at Preston's dad's old house that I talked him into. I rest in his arms until his alarm goes off. Then, our day begins, with him working on his computer and me taking care of Dad.

When the time for our date comes, after weeks of nursing my father back to health, I'm relieved to be taking a shower and getting dolled up.

The Versace glides over my skin, hugging my curves just like it did the first time I tried it on. A swipe of mascara and a dab of gloss and I'm set. This dress doesn't need anything more.

Preston wants me to meet him in the Ghost in ten minutes. I'm ready early so I go sink down into the leather seat, getting comfy for the long ride into the city. I turn on the dash and overhead twinkling star lights. I put on a little soothing classical pop music that lets me reminisce about that night at Brighton Manor.

Is this really my car? Every time I climb inside, I feel the thrill of that incredible date night.

Finally, I see him coming from the house. He wears dress pants and his navy suit jacket—the one that is perfectly tailored to his body.

He drives the Ghost out of the driveway but instead of turning right to head to the city, he turns left, the car climbing up the long drive toward Redmond Castle.

We're heading straight over the cobblestone road. The castle is the only thing at the end of this road. What in the world are we doing going up here?

"Babe," I say. "Where are we going?"

"Your present is up here," he says.

"At the castle?" I ask.

"Yes."

What could he possibly be hiding in the castle for me? It's been closed up for so long. The inside is icky, filled with spiderwebs and moths and maybe even mice. They never sent any money for upkeep, just threw it on the list for sale and left.

"I don't even think the electricity is turned on. What are we doing up here?"

"You ask too many questions, baby." He pats my thigh in that *conversation's closed* way he has. "Just ride."

As we pull up the drive, I spot white paper luminaries lighting our way. The same ones that were lining the drive to Brighton Manor. "Preston. It's beautiful."

We're at the meadow we had the picnic in that first night he was back in town. That must be where we're headed. How romantic! A picnic dinner. Although without my help, it's probably going to be cheese and crackers, but that doesn't matter. It's the thought that counts.

The nights are a little chilly for outdoor dining. I should have brought a coat. He pulls the Ghost in front of the stairs that lead up to the castle.

"We're not going in, are we? It's a mess in there. No one's been in there in ages."

He shoots me a look, one brow raised to the sky. "Jules."

"What?"

"I've got this under control."

"Okay."

"Sit tight."

I nestle back in the seat, waiting for him to come around and open my door.

Funny... the lights on the front porch are on. Somehow, he's managed to get the power turned back on.

He helps me from the car. "Ready for your present? It's inside."

"Yes," I say, but I'm not.

I was thinking we'd have a nice dinner in the city and he'd give me flowers. But now, I take his hand, holding it tight. I feel cold, icy nerves and excitement dancing through me, putting me on edge.

What waits for me inside that castle?

The door swings open, a man in a tux holding the gold handle. "Welcome, Ms. Verduce," he says.

"Hello," I say, then stare at Preston, hoping for some explanation. He just grins.

The floors are scrubbed, the hardwoods gleaming under new red Persian rugs. The chandeliers have been cleaned; sparkling light floods the entrance. Someone brought this place back to life. I can't believe it.

I try to form words for what I'm seeing, but all I manage is a breathy, "Preston…"

There's a man waiting for us in the foyer. He looks familiar. Holding his hand out to me, he says, "Tickets, please?"

Tickets? Then I remember where I know him from. He's the greeter from the Brighton Manor Ball. Preston hands him two golden tickets just like the ones from the ball that night.

Soft music starts just as we step into the ballroom. Am I dreaming? "Is that the Victory String Quartet?"

"It is." He grabs my hand, guiding me into the ballroom. The Quartet is set up on a small stage, playing just for us.

He pulls me in his arms for a dance. His arms are warm and strong, and they hold me on my weak knees. I stare up at him, speechless and overwhelmed. The music floats around us as we sway, wrapping us in a cocoon of soft sounds like we're the only two people in the world.

This moment, this, is the birthday gift. And it's the best gift I've ever been given.

Tears tickle at my throat, making my words low. "Thank you, Preston. I can't imagine a birthday more special than this."

"You deserve it, baby. You deserve it all." He leans down, kissing the top of my head. He takes my hand, twirling me around, then pulls me back into him.

"How did you manage this? What did the Redmonds say when you told them you wanted to borrow the castle for a night?" I ask.

His brow furrows. "I didn't."

"Then how did you pull this off?" I ask.

Our dancing slows to a stop.

Devil's smile all for me. "It's yours. I bought this for you."

"Huh?" I don't understand. A nervous giggle flutters through me. "What do you mean?"

He just stares down at me, smiling. "Exactly what I said."

My tongue is still frozen in my mouth, unable to reply. We never did have that follow up conversation after he gifted me the Ghost, did we? The one about not giving me elaborate gifts?

I'm so glad we didn't.

He bought me a *castle*. The very one I've dreamed of owning since I was a little girl. Every time I'd look up this hill and see the beautiful, abandoned building, it would break my heart.

Now, my heart feels so full it could burst.

Tears fill my eyes. "Preston..." My words trail off.

"It's yours. Part of the gift is the renovations. There's still work to be done upstairs but the main part of this floor is ready to be used. And you've already had two booking requests."

"Booking requests?"

"The Primetime Players have asked—well, demanded—that we let them host their annual Christmas Ball here." He nods over his shoulder at the band. "It was part of the deal in exchange for getting the Quartet here tonight, they had a hook-up, so I said yes. Didn't think you'd mind."

"I don't mind at all," I whisper, my eyes unable to stop gazing around at the carvings in the woodwork, the intricate details in the design. All...ours?

"The second request we got, I'm really hoping you'll say yes to," he says. "You'll be doing a solid for a good friend of mine. See, Cash proposed to his girl, Ella, and she's really sweet—you're going to love her—but she doesn't have much family around and he thought she might love her wedding more if they had it outside of the Village. You know, neutral turf."

"Neutral turf..." My words finally come, complete with a silly giggle. "Like a castle?"

"Exactly. Like a castle."

"Yes." I'm more than happy to add wedding and event planner to my list of part-time jobs. "Yes to everything!"

He exhales a sigh of relief. "Great. Now, I've just got one more question I'm hoping you'll answer yes to as well."

And the man of my dreams drops down to one knee before me.

My hands go to cover my gaping mouth.

He looks up at me, "Jules Verduce, I'm in love with you. I think I have been for a very long time now. Will you do me a favor?" He flashes his devilish grin, making my knees go weak. "Be my wife?"

He slips a little red leather box from the inside of his suit jacket. Gold letters swirl across the top. It's from Bachman's Jeweler. He goes to snap the lid open.

"Wait!" I put my hand over the box before he can show me what's inside. "Wait."

He gives me a panicked look. "What?"

"I want to tell you my answer before you show me the ring."

A flash of terror darts through his gaze. "Why?"

He's misunderstanding me.

"No," I shake my head laughing. "No, I mean—"

Color leaves his face. "No? Your answer is…no?"

"No, Preston! That's not my answer! I was trying to say, 'No, it's not what you're thinking.'" My palm goes to my forehead. "Gosh, I'm making a mess of this, aren't I? I mean, I just want to tell you *yes* before you show me the ring."

"Why?"

"Because it's going to be gorgeous and I'd never want you to think I was saying yes to the ring and not to you."

His brow furrows. "So, you're saying yes?"

A hysterical burst of laughter erupts from me. "Yes! A thousand times yes!" My shouts echo through the empty ballroom.

The Quartet stops playing, breaking out in cheers and claps and whoops.

"Thank God." He comes up off his knee. He opens the box, removes the ring and slips it on my finger.

A vintage floral halo diamond ring in white gold, the diamond is an offset square, surrounded by petal-like half circles, little points between them. The ring is everything I knew it would be. Nothing like what I would expect, and yet more "Jules-like" than anything I could have picked out for myself.

I stare down at the diamonds as they sparkle under the lights. "Oh, it's gorgeous, Preston! How do you always know what I love?"

"Honestly?" he shrugs. "I don't know how, but I do."

The music starts back up and we dance.

## 19

# Jules

Preston's voice calls up from the first floor. "Jules. Rich is here for you."

"For me?" I tug the last curl through my hair, unplugging the iron.

Makeup, on point. Hair, shining and voluminous thanks to the new balm Charlotte gave me. Clothes, chic but casual enough for a day of shopping. Yep—I look like a Beauty.

I head down the three flights of stairs from the master to the foyer. "Coming!"

We're staying in the Village this week so I can get the things I need for Ella's wedding. As much as I love Cedar Creek and the surrounding towns, the shopping is dismal. The catering, the flowers, the furniture, will all be from the city.

Richmond is standing by the front door, a massive stack of brown shipping boxes at his side. His elbow leans on the top of the pile. He's giving me an incredulous look.

"Jazzah." Rich uses his new British-ized nickname for me. He pats the stack of boxes. "Is this what I have to look forward to?" Rich is planning on proposing to his girl this weekend.

"If your place is as bare as Preston's, yes, you'll probably be having lots of packages being delivered," I laugh.

Preston runs a hand through his hair, eyeing all the crates. "I'd say thanks for dropping them off, man, but I think you've just made a world of work for me."

"Anything to keep the women happy," Richmond says.

The door opens and Rich moves out of the way to let Tess in.

"Hello!" She closes the door, looking at the boxes. "Ooh...your stuff came! Are these the paintings you got for the walls?"

"Not just paintings," Preston says. "Paintings, because she said my walls needed some color. Curtains, because we need privacy, and about a dozen different throw blankets and fancy cushions and pillows I've been told I'm not actually allowed to use or sleep on, to..." Preston holds up air quotes, "warm up the place."

"Yep. That sounds about right," Tess laughs. She grabs my hand. "Come on. The furniture guy is meeting us at the warehouse. I don't want to be late."

"See you soon," I say, reaching up on my toes and kissing Preston goodbye.

Bachmans don't rent. They own. The idea of wasting money on renting the tables and chairs we need for Ella and Cash's wedding at the castle was killing Tess, especially since more events have already been booked, including the Annual Bachman Ball next year. "Just look at it as a housewarming gift. You know—your husband bought you a castle for your birthday and we're helping to furnish it. Besides, we'll get just as much use out of it as you will."

Preston's helped me stake out the basement of the castle. We've created the perfect place to store everything that we'll be purchasing today. Knowing Tess, it's going to be a lot of stuff. I don't even want to see the bill.

Yeah—after pinching pennies and clipping coupons with my dad, I'm still floored by the amount of money Preston keeps in my bank account. Unlimited shopping?

That I'm quickly getting used to.

After a quick lunch of pasta and wine at Tess's favorite café, her driver takes us to the Meatpacking District to the warehouse. We've both opted for stylish sneakers to go with our outfits since we'll be logging quite a few miles, making the rounds on the concrete floors. Tess and I have a few things in common. Our names both end in the letter 's,' making it difficult for people to pluralize. We're both redheads.

And we both know what we want.

It only takes the two of us one hour to get everything we need, both for this event as well as the main elements we will need for future parties. Brown leather barstools, high top tables, easy-to-move narrow leather chairs and smaller round tables that are light to carry. She signs the order with a flourish as I thank her.

At home, I slip my shoes off, happy to see Preston's already assembled the table I ordered for the foyer. He's even hung the colorful piece of Impressionist art I chose for above the table. I stand back, taking in the difference from the bare gray walls that were here when I arrived.

Preston comes up behind me, slipping his arms around my waist. "I like it," he says, kissing my cheek.

I wrap my arms over his. "It looks nice, doesn't it?"

"How'd the shopping go?" His kiss moves down from my cheek to my neck.

"Good. But I've only stopped by to say a quick hi and grab the color swatches I forgot. I'm meeting Charlie at the florist at three." His kisses heat, the touch of a tongue as he moves lower. I know what he wants. But I really don't have time.

I turn, smiling. "Later. I promise. I've got to go."

"You're taking my driver, right?" he asks.

"We're taking Charlie's. She'll be getting off work from the jewelry store so I'm meeting her out front."

He repeats his rules for the hundredth time. "No walking around the city alone. No being in the city without a driver if you aren't with me. You're going to be—"

"A part of the family and that makes me a target for paparazzi and people that might want to hurt us," I finish for him. "I know, I know..."

"I'm serious, Jules. It's dangerous for you to be out there on your own." He kisses the top of my head. "I don't want anything to happen to you."

I don't bother reminding him that I've lived in the city alone before and handled myself just fine. He'll just tell me it's not the same thing as being a Bachman in the city. We've had this talk before.

"Okay, babe. I won't." I give him a quick kiss, wriggling out of his arms. I run upstairs to grab the forgotten color swatches. I throw on my shoes and grab my purse.

He swats my ass as I fly out the front door. "Be good," he growls.

"Always am!" I float along the sidewalk, visions of Lavender Veranda roses in my mind.

Ace is working the gate today. He greets me with a smile. "Miss Verduce. You look happy today."

"Probably because I'm shopping today," I laugh. "And I love it here in the Village."

"We can't wait to have you with us full-time."

Warmth fills me. Everyone's been so welcoming. "Thanks." I've not yet made the full move. Preston and I are half here, half in Cedar Creek. I like it like this, for now. I don't have to say goodbye to my hometown, and I have the city life that I love.

I try not to think about leaving the Creek. It's…hard.

The silver Saab is parked on the side of the road but Charlie's not here yet. Maybe she got hung up at work. I cruise down to the jewelry store and peek in the windows. She's helping a young couple, their gazes focused on the long length of diamond rings.

It doesn't look like she'll be able to get away any time soon. Feeling my gaze, she looks up at the window and waves. She gives the couple a smile, excusing herself and comes to the door. The little silver bell rings as she opens it, peeking her head out.

"I'm soooo sorry, Jules. I'm going to be here for at least another hour. You've got to go without me."

"I can try to reschedule?" I offer.

"Please? Mr. Chin does not reschedule. Not even for a Bachman. You'd better go, or we might miss out on the flowers we want."

"Okay, I'll send you pics."

"Thanks," she waves, calling over her shoulder as she leaves, "and take my driver!"

It's a beautiful day. The sunshine warms my skin, the cool air blows at my curls. The florist is only a few blocks away. I'd like a walk. I pass by the Saab, knocking on the window.

The driver rolls the window down. "Yes, ma'am?"

"Hi there. Charlie and I won't be needing a ride right now. She said she'll be done with work in about an hour. I just didn't want you to worry."

"Okay, thanks for letting me know." His dark brow knits. "So, you're going back to the Village, then?"

"Um, no. I'm just going for a walk. I'll be fine."

"Let me take you, it's no problem," he says, going to get out of the car to open my door.

"Really! I'm fine." I've lived in the city. On my own. I can walk a few blocks. I head in the direction of the florist before he can stop me. "Thank you!"

I'm enjoying the weather, cruising by the shops, doing a bit of window-shopping and having a moment of freedom. The crowds start to thin out as I get closer to the florist.

Voices creep up from behind me, walking a little too close considering how much sidewalk space there is.

"They let one out. I saw her coming from the gates. Went right by the driver and just kept walking on by herself," a gruff voice says.

"They never let them out on their own. Is this some kind of trap?"

The gruff one replies, "Nah. She's just gone rogue. Can't keep tabs on them all the time."

They're talking about...me. The hairs on the back of my neck stand on end and little sparks of fire lick at my cheeks.

The desire to run prickles at my heels. That's silly, right? They're just trying to scare me. I'm only a block from the florist. Determined to live my life, I hold my head up in the air and press on.

I walk a little faster.

As I pass by an alleyway, a hand grips my arm. *What the hell?* The gruff voice whispers in my ear, making my stomach clench with bile.

"Hey, pretty girl. Red on top, red on bottom?"

With horror, I turn to find a man with crooked, yellowed teeth and bloodshot eyes. His breath is foul and dirt is caked under his nails as he presses them into my arm.

It hurts.

"Let go of me." I tug away.

Now I'm halfway down an alley but the street is filled with people. Surely if I scream, someone will hear me and help me. But I don't need anyone. Not yet. I can fight for myself. "Let go now, or I kick you where the sun doesn't shine."

He just laughs.

"You know what they say about redheads, don't you? They put up a fight." A second voice comes around my other side. Another rough-looking man, bigger than the first, towers over me. "Feisty, I like it."

He clamps his hand over my opened mouth before I can scream. How is no one noticing what's happening to me? My mind spaces. I'm in serious danger.

"Get your hands off her." A deep voice booms through the alleyway. It's familiar but laced with a threat of violence I don't recognize. I tear against the man's hold, looking in the direction of the voice.

My knees go weak—it's Preston. My breath heaves and I just wait.

*Please, Preston.*

He barrels down the alley, a madman on a mission, ready to destroy everything in his path. The look on his face scares me, even though it's for my protection. I've never seen Preston like this. I knew a current of power and danger ran through him, always present under his cool façade. I've just never seen it in action.

Preston grabs the shoulders of the man with his hands on me, and I don't know if it's adrenaline or the fact that he's been bench-pressing me in my dad's living room when he's bored, but Preston tears the man from me and throws him to the ground without breaking a sweat.

The toe of Preston's boot makes contact with the man's ribcage, a cracking sound echoing through the alley. "Touch my woman, I'll break your hands." I have to look away as the heel of Preston's boot crushes the hand that a moment ago was covering my mouth.

The man rolls into a ball, moaning and clutching at his hand. Charlie's driver comes jogging down the alley. Preston shouts orders at him. "Get him in the car. Then call the others to find his friend. I want to know what they were doing with my girl."

I stand back, wrapping my arms around my middle. Were they just trying to scare me, or was I in real danger? Is this the second time Preston's saved my life?

Preston turns to me, hands on my shoulders, eyes locked on mine. "Are you okay? Did they hurt you?"

I shake my head. "I'm fine. I'm fine. He only had me for a minute before you came."

"Good." He kisses me. "I need to get this guy in the car. Stay put."

"Okay. I will."

"And Jules?"

"Yeah?"

Anger lights his eyes. "You and I are going to have a serious talk when we get home."

My ass clenches and my throat feels tight.

I swallow, hard.

His hand captures my chin between his thumb and forefinger. "I'm the head of this household."

I want to pull away, to tell him that his words are old-fashioned, outdated. But his gaze holds mine, his intentions burning through me. I knew what I was getting into when I chose him, when I chose this life.

When Preston gave me that ring, he gave me his promise to care for me, to protect me. And I don't get to pick and choose when I want that. It's a twenty-four-seven deal and right now, it's got me trembling.

"I know," I whisper.

"Do you?" Anger flashes in his irises. "Because what happened just now? You sure weren't acting like it."

"I just..." My words turn to dust on my tongue. There is no excuse. At least from his perspective.

"I made my expectations clear. And you promised me. How can I keep you safe when I can't trust you?"

"Don't say that, Preston. You can trust me. It was just a one-time thing. A mistake. I just wanted to go on my own."

"Don't you understand?" He releases my face, running a hand through his hair. "You can't go on your own anymore. That's not a choice you have."

"Fine." I cross my arms against my chest. I'm over the tension between us. I'm done with this conversation.

"Fine? That's all you have to say to me? Fine?" His tone goes low, his voice raking over hot coals. He's furious. Maybe even madder than he was when he first came into the alleyway.

"Sorry?" I take a step back from him. "I mean, what do you want me to say?"

He's on me in one second flat, one arm around my waist, one cupped around the back of my neck. "I want you to say that this will never, ever happen again. I want you to tell me that you will not put your life in jeopardy. I want you to tell me that you respect my position as head of this household, and as your husband-to-be, the head of you. I want you to tell me you accept that as a truth you're going to live by."

Am I really ready, willing, and able to submit myself to him? I stare into his eyes, and I know there is no choice for me.

The only choice for me is him.

"I accept." Unease twists around my spine, shivers dancing over me. What am I agreeing to?

And with those two words, his grip tightens on the back of my neck, his words fire against my skin. "You are mine. Soon you'll be my wife. And you need to know what that means."

The arm around my waist tightens until my breasts are flattening against him and my hip bones are digging into him. He bites at my ear, pain shooting through me. His fingers press into my neck. I can't move, he's got me trapped against him.

My inhales go shallow. I'm afraid to breathe or move or speak. What do I do?

Nothing.

That's not the question.

The question is...

*What is he going to do to me?*

## 20

# Preston

The men that attacked Jules in the alley are in the basement of our offices in the Village. I want to know why they put their hands on her. Then, I'll make sure they're no longer a risk to her.

Ever again.

First? I deal with my wayward bride-to-be.

Jules is dependable, someone you can trust. Generally, I can predict what she will do in any given situation. I guess that's why I had a nagging suspicious feeling in my gut when I kissed her goodbye today.

She's become more spontaneous since we've been together. Every time there's a decision to be made, she doesn't reach for her notebook to write out her pros and cons list. I'm all for it but not when it comes to her safety.

Where Jules' wellbeing is concerned? There is no room for spontaneity.

She promised she'd follow the rules. Then Charlie's driver called me to let me know Jules had passed on the ride to the florist. I was out of my house and on that sidewalk in two minutes flat, following her path from the tracker I installed on her phone.

My blood burns in my veins every time I think of that asshole's hands on my girl.

The sound of my phone ringing cuts through my thoughts. It's Eli, the head of our security detail. He quickly fills me in; this was no planned kidnapping attempt, just a couple of shady ass characters wanting to play cat and mouse for a moment. They saw an unattended Beauty and they wanted a piece, even if it was just to scare her a little, to have their hands on her...

Damn, there's that heat boiling through my system again. I tell Eli to take care of it. I don't trust myself to make quick, clean work of the job as Rockland demands of us. Besides, I'd much rather focus my attention where it matters most.

Jules.

I leave my phone on the foyer table, returning to our bedroom where I left her.

She's sitting on our bed, fully nude, her bare breasts rising and falling with each deep breath. There's a pretty pink curved vibrator cupping her sex, held on by an elastic band around her thighs and waist. It's made of silicone, hugging her from her entrance up over her mound. The entire piece vibrates when it's turned on, and a little tongue-like silicone flap moves back and forth with the push of a button.

I hold the remote in my hand. I've been pushing it on and off the entire time I've been on the phone. Whenever I get angry, thinking of her breaking my rule, putting herself in danger, I push it.

Her hands are folded in her lap, just like I told her to have them. Her eyes are wide and glassy, her face flushed, her bare breasts moving up and down with big heavy breaths. She's practically panting.

"Please," she whimpers. "I don't like it."

"I know you don't, baby. And I hope we don't have to go through this again."

I push the button. The buzz of the vibrator goes on and she gives a little gasp, her back arching, her fingers clenching together. Her toes curl into the brand new fluffy white rug she bought for the floor at the foot of the bed.

She's right—the rug really warms the place up.

I turn it off, taking a seat on the gray velvet couch she also bought. As she sits, whimpering and recovering, I run my hands over the fabric, enjoying the feel of it. "What a nice sofa you've picked out for our room. And very low arms. You know what this will be perfect for?"

"No."

I pat my empty thigh. "It's just right for putting you over my knee to punish you. I think I'll call this your spanking couch."

Moans of shame escape her pretty pout. I know she wants to bury her face in her hands, but she's not allowed to move them. She interlocks her fingers, squeezing.

"Why don't you come over here and we'll try it out?"

She doesn't want to.

"Bad girl." I push the button, turning the waggling tongue thing on high. Her back arches again, a strangled sound coming from the back of her throat. "I want you over my lap, now."

She pops up from the bed, her thighs pressed together as she waddle-walks over to me. I turn the vibrator off again and grab her hand, tugging her over to me till she's standing right in front of me.

"I love you, baby. And I want you to remember how uncomfortable that walk to me was the next time you want to walk somewhere by yourself."

"Yes, sir," she sniffles.

"Now lay over my lap."

She moves quickly, sliding over my lap. Her naked belly is warm against my legs. Her legs stretch out behind her, resting on the velvet sofa. I push the button, letting her body jolt over my lap.

"Oh! Oh...my...God..." Her words rise into a high-pitched whine. Her hips wiggle, wanting relief. I smooth my hand over her ass, cupping her cheek and giving it a squeeze.

"I love you and I want you to be a good girl and do what I ask of you." I spank her curves, right then left, right then left. The sting from my palm dances over her skin while the vibrator licks and hums over her sex.

"I want to come so badly." Her fingernails rake lines into the velvety fabric.

She's getting close. I turn it off, wanting to spank her more. I spank the center of her bottom, a hard spank that makes an angry red handprint pop up on her ass. She yelps, wiggling those pretty little hips.

"That huuurts," she whines.

"Good. Remember that the next time you want to disobey me and put yourself in danger." I spank her bottom with a nice rhythm, spanking right then left, over and over. She's whining into the cushion of the couch, clutching the edges of the seat.

My palm is stinging. Her ass must be on fire. Her bottom is getting red and hot and it's time to turn the vibrator back on. I push the button, adding orgasm denial to her punishment.

"Oh, babe! I can't take it, please. Turn it off."

"Bad girls don't get to beg for what they want." I spank her ass, hard, one cheek then the other. "They take what is given to them." I hold back a chuckle, rubbing my hand over her punished ass. "You want me to take this vibrator off of you?"

"Oh my God, yes, please!" She bucks her hips against me.

"Then get on your knees and show me how sorry you are." I hit the button, turning the vibrator off and toss the remote to the side. She lays over my lap, panting, trying to recover, her hands hovering around her spanked bottom, wanting to rub the sting from it.

She slips from my lap, kneeling on her white carpet. I reach down, snapping the vibrator off her. It drops to the floor and I pick it up, tossing it to the side with the remote. She's visibly relieved, her body relaxing.

I undo my pants, freeing my cock. It's ready for her.

Shyly, she scoots between my legs, taking my cock in her soft hand. I lean back, tucking my hands behind my head and watch. Her pretty pink pout wraps around the glistening head of my cock.

It feels so good, having her warm, wet mouth around me. Watching her take it heightens my pleasure. I love when she's my good girl and so docile like this. She's only this soft because she's been punished, brought to her knees in more ways than one.

Her fingers tighten around the base of my cock, her mouth moving further down my shaft.

"That's a good girl," I say. I slip my hand against the back of her head, guiding her further down. "Take me. Take all of me."

She sucks me off with her pretty little mouth, one hand cupping my balls, the other rubbing my shaft, just like I've taught her. The orgasm rises from my core, tightening everything. "That's it, baby. Just like that."

I wrap the hair on the back of her neck around my hand, giving it a tug. "There's a good girl. Suck me just like that. You're so good at this, baby. You make it feel so good."

I feel my seed rising in my shaft. I give a moan, shooting it all into her mouth. She takes down every drop, swallowing my hot come.

She pulls away, her lips bright red, her cheeks flushed from effort. She's got a shiny bit of come at the corner of her mouth. She reaches up to wipe it away. She looks to me for approval. "Did I do good?"

"You did so well. Come here, baby." I open my arms to her. She falls into them. I pull her onto my lap, wrapping my arms around her naked body. She winces as her punished bottom makes contact with my thigh. I hold her against me, rubbing her back and kissing her cheek and the top of her head.

"I'm sorry," she says sweetly, nestling her cheek against my chest. "I should have kept my promise."

"Thank you, baby. All is forgiven."

"Does that mean I get to come?" she asks. She gives a little sniffle.

"Not tonight. Tonight you'll be sleeping right next to me, naked with a red ass. That way anytime I get angry, thinking about you disobeying me, I can reach down and give it a nice spank."

She gives a sigh, but it's a happy sigh and she snuggles harder against me.

## 21

### Jules

My heels click over the hardwood floors, clipboard in hand as I make my way through the foyer. Different heights of white pillar candles, check. Vases filled with pampas grass and burnt orange and burgundy roses—yeah, I missed out on Mr. Chin's Lavender Verandas because of my little incident that day in the city, but the bouquets are gorgeous—dotted with sprigs of baby's breath.

Heading to the dining room I flip to the next page. Drinks and apps. Okay, we've got the Redmond's old buffet turned into the perfect bar, I've got a champagne tower set up and ready to flow on the big night—cheesy, I know, but I love them—and a couple heavy mahogany buffets set around the room that will be spread with sweets and savories for nibbling during cocktail hour.

Now for the ballroom. Ella wanted to avoid the stuffiness of a sit-down dinner. Instead we've opted for high top tables and barstools dotting the edges of the great room. There'll be a buffet of meats and veg to choose from. People can mingle and dance and eat and drink as they please.

Ella's chosen to skip the rehearsal dinner, opting for a short ceremony and a casual reception, no formal daddy-daughter dance or anything like that. I think she's made good choices. She has little family and few friends coming and having the ceremony be more of a party, I think she'll feel right at home among her new family.

And what girl doesn't want to get married in a castle? *Am I right?*

I peek into the kitchen. The Bitch'en Kitch'en was on board with catering the reception but when the liaison from the restaurant came out and saw our brand-new commercial kitchen, they had one stipulation. All the cooking would be done on site. Heavenly scents come from the stove and ovens, several cooks bustle about in black aprons, laughing and teasing as they do their prep work for tomorrow.

Moving through the open doors out to the veranda, I find the outdoor bar and dance floor ready to go, the final strings of lights being hung.

I clip my pen to my board. I think I've got all my bases covered. Marrying a Bachman, I don't have a financial need to work, but I have a personal need to be filled. Paid or not, I love to work. And there is no greater joy for me right now than to make Ella's special day perfect.

I check my watch, a slender little gold number gifted to me by Preston. Five minutes until my bride is due. Making my way through the foyer, I inhale the scent of the roses.

The bell rings right at two, a lovely melody of bells chiming through the air. I open the door. "Ella!"

Her hair hangs in dark waves over her shoulders, a short, deep blue dress hugs her curves perfectly. Her cheeks are flushed, her eyes wide with excitement as she takes in the foyer. I grab her in a hug.

"Welcome to your wedding."

And she bursts into tears.

Um…crying bride? Not what I was expecting. I wrap an arm around her shoulders, ushering her into the castle. "Come in, come in. Oh honey, what's the matter?"

"I don't know," she says, dabbing at her eyes, trying to save her melting mascara. "I've been crying all week."

"Tell me." I sit her down in the parlor where I've already got a tray of tea waiting for us. "Are they happy tears or sad tears?"

"I don't know," she wails, crying into the napkin I've handed her.

"Well, it's a big day. It's a lot to take in. You might be a little overwhelmed by everything."

She sniffs, shaking her head. "Nooo. I don't think it's that. I'm so excited! And you've got everything perfect and it's just what I wanted and…and…and…" She breaks out into a fresh round of sobs.

There's only one time of the month I cry this many tears for no reason. A solid half pound of chocolate and a bottle of Ibuprofen is also usually involved. "Um…Ella?"

"Yes," she says.

"I'm not trying to pry, but, um. Is it that time of the month?" I ask.

"What time?" Her eyes widen. "Oh—yes, I um…I ah…"

Her words trail off. Her dark brows knit together, her pretty pink lips moving as she looks up at the chandelier, counting in her head.

She stops. Looks at me. Swallows hard and starts to count again.

*Uh. Oh.*

"So. Ah. Um. Err…"

I put my hand over her trembling fingers. "It's okay. Just breathe, Ella. We'll figure this out."

"Figure it out…okay…yeah. That sounds…"

My bride goes from blushing to pale. The color drains from her face. Completely.

I'm saying her name, "Ella. Ella." But she's not looking at me. She's looking past me.

This isn't good. This really isn't good.

She takes a deep breath and starts to sway.

"Oh my gosh, Ella." I grab her shoulders, laying her down on the small velvet chaise she's seated on. It just happens to be a Victorian "fainting couch." And my bride has just fainted.

I stand, making sure she's lying comfortably. "Okay. I'm calling Preston. Right now. He'll bring Cash."

Ella's fiancé, Cash, is out with Preston; they're having coffee down on Main Street. I explain that Ella has passed out. They're on their way.

I kneel by Ella, waiting for Cash. "He's on the way, honey. Just hang on."

"Hmm?" Her lids finally flutter open.

"Thank God." I smooth her hair back from her face. "Cash will be here any minute."

A moment later the men burst through the door and Cash replaces me, kneeling at Ella's feet. "Babygirl. What happened?"

"I don't really know." Ella looks to me for an explanation.

She wants *me* to tell him? I hold in a groan. How does this task possibly fall on my shoulders?

I'm just supposed to be planning the wedding.

I take a deep breath. "Okay. So here's what happened. Ella was crying—"

"Crying?" Cash's ice blue eyes lock on mine. "Why was she crying?"

"Ah, she wasn't sure. So I suggested that maybe it was, you know..." Do I have to spell it out for them? The men stare at me, neither one having any idea what I'm talking about. Yes, I guess I do. I lower my voice to a whisper. "I asked her if it was her...time of the month?"

Ella buries her face in her hands. "That's right. Oh, how did I forget that?"

"She was counting backward. And then she went white as a sheet and passed right out," I say.

Cash looks to Ella. "Is there something you need to tell me?"

She shakes her head. "I don't know. I mean, I won't know for sure until we take a test, but...maybe?" She shrugs.

Now Cash goes white. I swear if one more person passes out...

Cash is still kneeling before Ella, holding her hands in his. She's leaning down, whispering something to him that makes him smile. This couple obviously needs a moment alone.

I say, "Preston. Why don't you go in the kitchen and get Cash a cup of coffee? I'll run down to the drugstore and get what Ella needs."

"Right." Preston hops to. "Coffee. On it."

We leave the parlor. Preston pulls the doors closed behind us. He leaves me with a kiss, off to waste some time in the kitchen.

"Hey, babe?" I call out as I grab my purse from beside the door.

"Yes?"

"Don't get in their way, okay? They don't need a taste tester." Preston's known for eating half of dinner just by picking at it while I'm cooking.

He gives me a military salute. "Aye, aye, Captain."

My walk down to the drugstore gives me time to contemplate Ella's situation. If this test is positive, it's obviously going to be quite a shock for her. I don't know how late she is, but when she was counting it out, it was clearly enough to make her pass out.

My hand goes to my flat, empty belly.

Last week when we were shopping for plants, we picked out this adorable little succulent. Something that didn't need much care to survive. Preston made a joke about it being our baby.

I must have grimaced when he said it because he gave pause. "Don't you want kids?" he asked.

"Do you?" I asked.

"Hell, yes," he said, a huge grin on his face. "I want at least three little redheaded girls just as sweet as you."

I almost dropped our plant baby when he said it.

He's ready for kids? Now? And not just one, but *three?*

Thinking of Ella's possible pregnancy, I can't help but have visions of those three little girls he mentioned. They're dancing through my head in little pink tutus. Baby girl names float through my mind.

Pippa and Emma. Sophie or Mia...

*Jules. Get it together.*

We are not ready for kids. I am not ready for kids. And I don't know when I will be. You can't just *have* kids. *Am I right?* There's planning involved. You've got to find the perfect OB-GYN. Start prenatal vitamins. Get that college savings account going.

You can't just get pregnant.

*Am* I right?

I think of the happiness on Preston's face when he mentioned his three little dream girls.

Maybe some things, you can just let...happen...

I get the test and grab her a box of chocolates and a few feminine supplies. Just in case. Ella's waiting for me on the stoop, Cash's arms wrapped around her waist. "Here." I hand Ella the bag.

She gives me a thank you squeeze, and they disappear upstairs.

Preston's waiting for me in the parlor, a plate of canapes in his hand and a guilty look on his face.

I eye the plate.

"What?" he shrugs.

"I said no taste testing, Preston." I reach for one of the treats.

"They made me. I swear."

I pop it in my mouth. "Whoa. That's delicious."

"Hey, this whole thing with Ella and Cash got me thinking." He puts the plate down, wrapping his arms around my waist. "Have you given any more thought to my triplets?"

"Wait, now they're not only three kids, they're triplets?" I laugh.

"You like efficiency." He kisses me. "Get it all done at once."

"I don't even know." I think of my own mother and the heartache we've all just gone through. I think of my pros and cons list. I think of the succulent on my windowsill with three dead leaves. "I think we'll stick with the plants for now."

He shoots me a curious look, but we're interrupted by Ella and Cash coming down the stairs. She's laughing and he's got his arm around her.

"What's the verdict?" Preston calls to them.

"Preston!" I hiss, elbowing him in the ribs. "Keep it in the courtroom. They'll tell us if they want."

Ella says, "False alarm!"

Cash says, "One day, but today is not that day. I want my bride all to myself for at least a year," he says, kissing her.

"Can I chat with you for a minute, Jules." Ella tugs me down the hall to fill me in. She thanks me for the foresight to buy the tampons. Apparently, as soon as she went to take the test, it came. We both complain a little about how unfair it is to have her period for her wedding. She says, "I'm so sorry I fainted on you! I always get a little lightheaded around this time of the month."

When she sees the rest of the venue and has eaten half the box of chocolates, she's completely consoled. Happy that she's happy, I go home at the end of the day feeling confident that the wedding is going to be just perfect.

The Ghost is in the driveway when I get home, Preston standing beside the open passenger door. "Get in."

"Where are we going?" I slip into the leather seat.

I was thinking I'd come home and cook dinner and get a good night's sleep for tomorrow. But he's got a smile on his face that tells me I'm in for a much better time than that.

"Lions Gate." He kisses me and closes the door. "You've been working so hard, I thought you could use a break."

The idea of an evening at a quaint little B&B before the Bachmans come rolling into town at noon tomorrow sounds amazing. "Yes, please."

"I've already ordered dinner to be delivered. It'll be waiting for us in the room."

"What'd you order?"

"Your favorite. Italian wedding soup and that crusty bread you like."

Soup. Something light. That means he must have sexy plans for afterward. Yay. The thought reminds me that it's time to take my birth control pill.

The room is gorgeous. I love the antique theme, the floral-patterned wallpaper, the solid wood furniture, the brass bed, the lacy curtains. I sit on the bed, feeling the soft quilt.

He takes my bag from his arm, handing it to me. "I packed everything you need."

"Thank you." I root through the bag looking for my pills. Not here. "Preston. I think you may have forgotten my birth control."

"Did I?" he asks.

"Should we go back and get it?" I recheck all the pockets of my bag. They're not here.

He takes the bag from me. "You're not going to find them in there."

"Preston?"

He takes my hands. "I didn't bring them."

"Okay." This is strange. "Can I ask why?"

He pulls me into him. My head rests on his chest. He leans down, nuzzling my ear. "Because I want to get you pregnant. I want my baby inside you."

His sexy words thrill me, waking a thrumming in my core, making my uterus go all heavy and achy.

My mind fights with my body, listing all the reasons why we can't do this.

"But you have to plan these things. You can't just…" I go to list all my reasons, but his mouth is on my neck, his teeth nipping at my skin and I'm melting against him. I catch my breath and try again. "Preston. You have to map this stuff out, point by point. We need at least one pros and cons list."

He chuckles against me, his teeth at my earlobe. "Pros and cons list. You're cute." His fingers dip under my skirt, teasing me over my panties. He lashes my earlobe with the tip of his tongue. "Pro. I want my baby," he slips my panties to the side, pushing a finger past my tight entrance, "inside of you."

"You know it takes time, right? It's not usually the first time—" He adds a second finger to the first. "Ah...*oh.*" My body has all but pushed my mind entirely out of the equation. Reason wars with emotion and finally a sliver of it wins out.

"Preston. We have a wedding to plan. What about what Cash said? Having a year with just the two of us. To get to know one another better."

He stops his playing just long enough to shoot a brow at me. "I feel like I know you inside and out. I finish half your sentences."

"True," I say, feeling the exact same way.

He turns his attention back to my body. "If I get my way, it will happen tonight. So I have to do all the things I want to do to you, just in case."

"What could you want to do to me that you couldn't do to me if I was pregnant?" A thrill runs through me.

"Everything," he says. "Once my baby is inside you, you're not going to be allowed to move a muscle. And it's gentle sex all the way until the baby is born." The thought of having his babies, being under his loving protection during my pregnancy, warms me all the way through.

A giddy excitement about the future bubbles up. I want to give a nervous laugh but he's touching me and the laughter gets lost in my throat. I ask, "What are you going to do to me first?"

"I want you in that very first bra and panty set I gave you. But this time, I want you in the stockings, too." His lips trail down my neck. "Then, I'm going to tie you to the bed. And do what I want."

My belly flips. Being tied down isn't something I've ever done. The idea of having no control, not being able to move my hands, has my breaths coming quicker.

He sends me to change, anticipation blooming in my belly. There's a sitting room attached to the bedroom. My lingerie is laid out. The triangle lace bra, the still very much missing-a-crotch panties, and now the silk stockings and garter belt.

I've never worn a garter belt. I've never even tried this one on. I hope I can get it figured out. Stepping out of my clothing, I stare in the mirror fully nude. It makes me remember that night in the Village when Preston made me watch him in the mirror while he brought me to orgasm.

My already throbbing nipples tighten. As the lace of the bra brushes over them, they're so sensitive, a shiver jolts through me. I step into the panties, pulling the bands high up over my hips.

I turn back and forth in front of the mirror. Damn. Looking good. Now for the stockings. I shimmy the garter belt over my hips, pulling it up to my waist so the little pink flower rests just below my navel.

I perch on the edge of a seat, rolling the silky stockings slowly so they don't get a run in them. I slip my toes into the end, carefully rolling them up my calf, making sure the black line riding up the back is nice and straight. The lacy band at the top of the thigh high holds the tights up but I still figure out how to clasp the plastic hooks into the lace.

I slip back into my black patent leather heels, leaving the rest of my clothing behind.

Six months ago? I'd have stayed in this room for at least another ten minutes, too shy to show off. Now? Preston makes me feel so damn sexy, I strut right out to the center of the room, showing off the curve of my calves, the rise of my breasts, the fullness of my ass.

The look on his face melts the crotchless panties right off my body.

What does he have in store for me?

## 22

# Preston

She takes my breath away. I can't tear my gaze from that soft span of naked skin between the tops of her thigh highs and her garter. The stockings take me over the edge, my balls riding high and tight just from looking at her.

I tear off my shirt, and her eyes dance over my bare chest. Leaving on my jeans, I go to her, wrapping my hands around her ribcage. "Come here."

She tilts her chin up, offering her mouth for kisses, but she's not in charge. I lead her to the bed, lying her down over the soft covers. I run my hands over her arms, bringing them up and over her head. I slip the fur-covered handcuffs from where I've hidden them under the pillow.

She watches wide-eyed as I slip her wrists into the cuffs, linking them around a bar of the headboard. At the sound of the clink of them closing, her teeth sink into her bottom lip. There's a silk blindfold under the other pillow. I slide it out, letting her watch.

"Oh! Is that for—"

"Shh..." I take the blindfold, slipping it around her eyes and tie it behind her head.

She tugs at the cuffs, twisting a bit to feel the hold of her restraints. She's so beautiful like this, out of control. I slip her shoes from her feet. Wrapping a silk tie around each of her ankles, I secure those to the bars of the footboard.

I crawl over her, leaning my mouth down to hers. "Now when you're all tied up like this, baby, you say 'yes sir' to get what you want. Do you understand?"

"Yes, sir."

"Good girl." I drag a finger from her lips, over her chin, down the slope of her neck, dipping below the thin strap of her bra, sliding it from her shoulder. The triangle falls away from her breast, exposing her peaked nipple.

I give it a flick.

"Oh!" She jerks as the pain shoots through her, her wrists tugging at her cuffs. I flick my tongue over her sweet bud, then take it in my mouth, sucking and nibbling it. I kiss my way down her torso, nuzzling her sweet pussy over her panties.

"Do you want my tongue on you, baby?"

"Yes, sir."

"Good girl." I love to hear the obedient words roll off her tongue. Parting the lacy sides of her crotchless panties, darting my tongue inside of her, I swirl around her entrance, tasting her. Dipping my fingers inside her, I gather her arousal.

I move up toward her face, holding my fingers to her lips. "Taste yourself," I say.

Her face flushes and she shakes her head. "I can't."

I slip my fingers in her mouth. "Taste."

She lets out a low moan, her tongue hot and wet against my fingers. I pull my fingers from her mouth, replacing them with my tongue. I swipe against hers, tasting her again. As I kiss her, my fingers find her once more, teasing her sweet little bud.

My touch makes her hips buck against me. I know her so well; I can tell by the cadence of her breath, she's already close to climax.

"Don't come," I say. "Not until I give you permission."

"Yes, sir...but...ah...I can't—"

"Don't be a bad girl. Do what I say, or I'm going to have to flip you over and take my belt to your ass for disobeying." Moving the pad of my thumb to her clit, I push two fingers inside her tight opening, stroking that velvety spot inside her that guarantees her a toe-curling orgasm.

"Not fair, Preston," she whimpers. "How do you expect me to—oh!"

"Preston?" I cut off her words with a sharp smack on her thigh.

"Sorry, sir. I just. I'm not sure..."

I pump and massage and kiss her neck till her sex clenches around my fingers and her voice sings into my ear, "Oh, my God. Oh, my God!"

She comes, hard, her body wanting to curl around mine, but the restraints hold her back.

"Naughty, naughty girl. You came and I didn't give you permission." I slip the blindfold from her eyes. She stares at me with a hint of fear and shame in her blue eyes. "I'm going to have to punish you with my belt."

Her lips form a little "o" of surprise. She didn't think I was serious. Untying the silks that hold her ankles, I grab her hips, flipping her over. The cuffs around her wrists twist with her. I reach up to make sure there's enough slack there for her comfort.

Then, I take in my beauty.

The lacy band of her bra wraps around her upper back. The garter belt is cinched around her slender waist, the black satin ribbons reach down to meet the tops of the lace of her stockings. And her ass—it's fully encased in all her finery, ready for me.

Kneeling between her thighs, I stroke her full curves, massaging her flesh. She moans as I part her cheeks, feasting my gaze on that tight little hole I'm going to claim tonight. I lean down, tonguing her bud.

She gasps. "You can't do that...Oh!"

She likes it, just like I knew she would. My fingers dig into her flesh, parting her further as I tease her ass with my mouth. Sitting up, I give her ass a smack. "Ready for my belt, baby?"

"No, sir." She shakes her head, burying her face in the pillow.

The metal buckle of my belt clinks as I undo it. I slip the leather through the loops, the swishing sound making her ass cheeks clench together and she moans.

Doubling the belt over, I drag it over the fullest part of her curves. "Relax, baby." I scoot further down the bed toward her feet, giving me more room to maneuver the belt. Lifting it, I bring it down across the center of her right cheek, gliding it over her thighs after it lands.

She gives a moan of pleasure, the sting of pain, the feel of the leather gliding over her skin making her fingers clench at the cuffs around her wrists.

"Ask me for another one, baby." I move the belt to her left side, dragging it over her ass.

Shame fills her voice. "I have to ask for it?"

"Yes."

Her words come breathy and sexy, and my cock goes hard between my thighs. "Please sir, can I have your belt?"

"Good girl." I lift the belt again, striking her left cheek. As I move the belt down from her curve, a pretty pink stripe rises on her flesh. "There's a beautiful mark from my belt across your ass cheek. Let me get a picture."

I reach for my cell phone on the nightstand.

"No...no." She moans.

"Just for me, baby." I stare down at the full cheeks of her ass, the lace and ribbons, the pink lines growing rosier over her curves. "No one will ever see it."

"Okay?"

I take the picture. One I know I'll never get tired of looking at. I toss my belt to the side, grabbing the lube from the nightstand. Parting the cheeks of her ass, I squeeze the tube, lining the crack of her ass with the cold jelly.

She gives a little shiver. "Oh, that's cold. What are you doing?"

Massaging the lube between her cheeks, I focus on her pretty little rosebud, lubing the tight muscles. "I'm getting you ready for me to take you." I press the tip of my finger past her unwilling muscles. "Here."

"I don't know..." She turns her face, her flushed cheek on display. "Am I ready?"

We've been playing whenever we spend the night at my place in the Village, using plugs to get her ready for my cock. "You're ready."

I push my fingers further into her. She gives a wiggle and a moan. I've got her body ready. Squeezing a dollop of jelly in the palm of my hand, I stroke the full length of my cock, ending with a swirl around the head. I grab her hips, guiding her ass up in the air, bringing her to her knees. I unclasp the cuffs so she can press her palms into the bed to balance her weight.

She spreads her thighs. I stroke her back, pressing my palm between her shoulder blades, pushing her chest down onto the bed.

I line the head of my cock up against her slick muscle. I'm pushing into her but her body fights back. "Relax baby, take a deep breath."

An inhale shudders through her. "Okay. I'm trying."

I push harder, finally making some headway. Terrible pun but—*oh shit*. Euphoria lights my core as the tight warmth of her wraps around my cock. "How does that feel?"

"Unh...it feels strange but good."

I move in further.

"Oh, I feel so full..."

Holding her hips tighter, I force my way deeper inside her. I love the tightness of her ass, the feeling of taking her yet another place no other man has ever touched. She's all mine and I'm claiming this ass.

I give her ass a nice spank, making her moan. Rolling my hips, I build up a rhythm as I reach around her hip. My fingers dip down, gliding over her slick sex. She's so wet and when I touch her, her ass clamps down harder on my cock.

It feels fucking amazing and the feeling rushes up my cock, diving deep into my balls. Everything tightens, pulling together, my seed ready to burst. My fingers move in time with her hips as she rolls them against me. I'm moving into her, she's pushing back into me. My hand works her sex and moments later, she gives a moan that lets me know she's close.

"Come on, come on, baby." I've got to come. "Come on, baby."

Finally, she reaches back for me, clutching me with her fingers. She locks down on my cock and I fucking explode. The relief rushes through me, the buildup of tension dissipating as I lean down over her, my chest resting on her back, our naked slick skin pressing together.

I kiss the back of her neck, then collapse on my right side, pulling her into a spoon hold. She nestles against me, letting her breaths slow. I smooth her damp hair back from her face, tickling my fingers down her ribs as I kiss her shoulder.

"I love you, baby," I whisper against her ear.

She reaches back, gliding a hand over the back of my head. "Love you too, babe."

We shower then fall back into the bed afterward. This time, we make love. Long and sweet and when I come, I let my seed burst inside of her, free to go where it wants to, to do what it wants.

I hold her naked body against mine. Her head rests on my chest. I run my fingers up and down over the back of her arm. I feel so close to her, I don't want anything between us. I want to tell her about that night.

I start with, "Since my baby is currently growing inside you—"

She laughs. "Babe, I don't think that's possible."

"Still, I love you and I don't want any secrets between us."

"Secrets?" Her nose crinkles. "I don't like that word."

"Sorry. Not secrets, it's just, I want to tell you what happened that night. About the arrest. I don't want that hanging between us."

"I really don't mind. I promise." She glances up at me from under her lashes. "But it would make me feel even closer to you to know what happened."

I lean up on an elbow so I can face her. "It was my eighteenth birthday that night."

"Our night?" she asks, surprised.

"Yes. That's why I had you leave me at the gate. My friends were at one of our buddies' houses just outside of town, waiting for me to come party with them."

"You couldn't have brought me with you?" she jokes.

"It was all guys. You'd have hated it. On my walk there, though, all I wanted to do was go back to you."

"Oh, that's sweet," she says.

That's where the sweetness of the story ends. "When I got there, I found the sheriff waiting for me." I remember my heart stopping in my chest at the sight of the car.

I'd done nothing wrong, yet somehow, I knew the flashing blue, red and white lights were there for me.

"No…really? What happened? Why?" She sits up, wrapping her arms around her knees.

"Someone at the bonfire in the woods saw me get into your car. They ratted you out to your dad, telling him I hopped in your car and we snuck out of Cedar Creek. Your dad already hated me. Worried about you, he called the police, saying you were missing. That you were with me."

"My dad did that?" Her brows knit together. "But I snuck in that night. His bedroom door was shut. He was sleeping."

"I don't think so. I think he just didn't want you to know. He told the sheriff one other thing."

"What?" she asks.

"He told him that you were a minor." I swallow back my anger. "And that I was of age."

"Oh my gosh." Her hands flutter to her mouth. "He didn't!"

"He did."

"But we didn't even do anything! I mean there was a little kissing and touching…"

"And skinny-dipping," I say, fondly.

"Yeah. And the whole part where you saved my life. He's going to feel so ashamed when he hears you literally saved his daughter and in return, he calls the sheriff..."

"I never should have had you in that water," I say.

"It was fun. We were young and being spontaneous. Anyway, what happened after that?"

"I was arrested. They took me down to the county jail and booked me in for the night while they figured out what was going on, what the real story was."

"Oh no. I'm so sorry. I had no idea," she says.

"It's not your fault. That's why I didn't want to tell you. I knew you'd feel responsible."

"I know..."

I just want to be done with this story. "Thank God for Rich. He was in the drunk tank that night, some kind of boys camping trip with buddies from England who'd come into town. Too much drinking and he ended up streaking through the town. We got to talking and I hadn't laughed that hard in a long time. When Rockland came to bail him out, he bailed me out too. After I left the jail that night, I never heard another word about the arrest as far as charges went, and that was the end of it. Rockland took care of it."

"I'm so glad. I feel terrible for what my dad did—"

"Don't. Honestly, it's over. I just wanted you to know.

She reads my face. "There's more to the story, isn't there?"

I hate to tell her the rest, I know she's going to feel guilty. But I want to tell her the full truth.

"The college I was going to in the fall found out I'd been arrested. I lost my full ride scholarship, and I got kicked off the baseball team at that school. In the end, I couldn't afford the college on my own. And the college wasn't the only one who knew about my arrest. My dad found out. He was furious. Called me just to tell me that would be the last time we spoke. Nice, right?"

"That's terrible. I would never stop talking to my kids. No matter what they did," she says. I agree. She asks, "How did you end up getting your degree? How did it all work out?"

"I had stayed in touch with Richmond. He got me started working for the Bachmans at night, and I went to school during the day. I didn't get much sleep, but I had enough money to pay for class with savings left over. After being arrested, I wanted to know the ins and outs of the criminal justice system. I wanted to be able to protect myself and the people I loved. I got my degree in law. The day I joined the family was the same day I became a lawyer for Bachman and Bachman."

Her nose crinkles adorably. "So it all worked out? Kind of?" she asks.

"It all worked out better than I could have planned," I say, leaning down and kissing her.

She gives an adorable little growl. "Still, I can't believe my dad did that. I'm so mad. And I was the one that let you in my car."

"Listen. He was looking out for you. Was it overkill? Yes. Did I suffer because of it? Yes. Did it all work out? Absolutely." I think of that day at their kitchen table when he looked at me and said, *I owe you an apology, son.* "He's apologized and he's been through so much. I say we just let it go. Okay?"

"Thank you for telling me." She curls up beside me.

And all is well.

## 23

J ules

The family has a private, Bachmans only, ceremony for Cash and Ella to exchange their wedding vows. I was so busy putting out little last-minute fires that I didn't have time to feel left out. Besides, in a few short months I'll have my own and I'll know what all the fuss is about.

They begin to arrive at the castle for cocktail hour. I remember most of the people from the dinner they threw me at the Village, and I have a great time re-meeting everyone. The Beauties surround me, wanting to know what my plans are.

Charlie asks, "Have you found a dress?"

"Are you going to get married here too?" Charlotte wants to know. "I'd love to get married in a castle. How romantic!"

Tess leans in. "What color theme are you going to go with. You know, redheads can have pink. It's a lie that they can't. You just need to go lighter with blush or go bold with it."

I appease them with a simple, true answer. "I'm not even thinking about my wedding until Ella's is over." They have to agree with me, and they turn their attention back to the bride.

Ella looks like a princess, dancing across the floor with her husband. Her smile shines like the sun, warming the entire room. She's worn her hair down, flowing over her bare shoulders in her simple strapless white dress. A sparkly veil hangs down her back.

When the Beauties asked her what her something blue was, she said, "My husband's eyes." Cash holds her in his strong arms, looking striking in his white tux. His gaze never leaves her face.

We serve the cake, double chocolate ganache. The couple feeds one another dainty bites and a cheer erupts. Empty champagne flutes are passed around, each guest filling their own from my fountain.

Preston comes up behind me, wrapping his arms around my waist. "You did a great job, baby. I can't believe this was your first wedding. You're a pro."

I hold my arms over his. "Thanks. It was fun. And it didn't hurt that I had a castle of my very own, did it?"

"I'm afraid the castle might have been a mistake," he says.

"Why?" I turn to catch his eye over my shoulder.

"Because. How on earth do I ever top the very first birthday gift I ever gave you?"

That makes me laugh.

The music changes to Pop dance tunes. My dad and Erin hit the floor, doing silly dances together that I'm too young to know the names of. My dad's totally healed. Erin has him on a plant-based diet and he's even off his cholesterol medicine.

They've been spending more and more time together. They're ready to move in together. And, I know, Preston's tired of commuting on the days that he needs to be in the office. He needs to get back to the city.

But what about my little town? My castle? I'm torn between two places.

"Preston," I say. "When are we moving to the Village?"

"If it were up to me? Yesterday," he laughs. "Just kidding. But seriously, we need to get you moved into my place. It's going to be our place pretty soon. You can come visit your dad anytime, and when you have events, we'll spend weekends at the castle."

It's a good plan. I think of what he told me last night...about what my dad did, about Preston's arrest and how it affected his life. Sure, it all worked out in the end, but he went through some heartbreak first. No wonder he held so much resentment for Cedar Creek. Why would he want to spend another moment here?

He's done so much for me...

It's time I make a sacrifice for him.

Even if that sacrifice brings tears to my eyes.

I turn around, facing him. "You know I'm obsessed with this castle and I love my new job running it, but if you don't want to have anything to do with this place, I understand." I run my hand over his chest. "I'm ready and willing to give it up. Beau can take over the events here. We can move to the Village. And if my dad wants to visit, we can always get them a hotel in the city."

He furrows his brow. "Really?"

"Yes."

He gives a big sigh, running a hand through his hair. "That might be a problem." His brows raise and he shakes his head.

It's not the reaction I'm expecting. "Why?"

"Because. The family's fallen in love with this place."

The Bachmans have a hidden village in the city, a mountain retreat, a mini-city in Connecticut and their own private island in Greece. What on earth would they want with my sleepy little town? I ask, "What are you talking about?"

"It's quiet out here, but not too far from the city. The perfect getaway. Rockland's already talked to the Elders. Half were ready to sell their places and move on, the others ready to retire and just live here peacefully. It looks like we're taking over the town."

"Taking over the town…" I try to picture the classy Bachmans gliding down Main Street in their couture and red soled Louboutins.

"Well, we'll make it our own, of course. There's going to be a bar and a club and an all-night breakfast place. We'll open it up to tourists, make the empty houses vacation rentals, or overnight stays for visitors who are having events at the castle."

I picture this place being overrun by the colors and energy of The Primetime Players. The laughter, the costumes, the parties they'll throw when they have their Christmas Ball here. We can host overnight guests that are having events at the castle.

"That would be amazing," I say. "Can we really pull that off? I mean, is that really what you want?"

"If you're happy. I'm happy. Besides, this place is kind of growing on me. I've got the old dudes I drink coffee with on Saturday mornings." He meets the Elders for coffee every weekend we're in town. "And I can't leave my love."

"Your love?" I say, raising my brow.

"The Alpha Romeo I'm rebuilding with Beau," he says.

I remember the car they've been tinkering with. "No, we can't leave her behind, can we?"

I'm so glad that the three most important men in my life are all getting along. Beau and Preston have bonded over car talk. Dad's joined us for game night. All is well. I'm relieved he doesn't want to leave the Creek behind.

"Are you sure?" I ask.

"Yes." He adds, "Rockland and Tess already bought the Henderson's cabin, the one back by the river? They're turning it into a weekend getaway, a little love nest. So, it's done."

"The country mouse marries the city mouse," I say, reaching up to kiss him.

He growls into my ear. "The city *lion* is going to eat this little country mouse all up."

"Babe. I'm working." Giggling, I shrug from his hold.

"Look around. Everything is perfect. All because of your hard work. No one will miss you for a few minutes."

Grabbing my hand, he pulls me down the hall. We bump into Rockland and Tess. Tess's usually perfect hair looks a bit disheveled and Rockland's tie is crooked.

"Oh, hi!" Tess pats at her hair, trying to smooth it. "Jules! You've outdone yourself with this wedding. I don't know that I've ever seen Ella this happy."

Rockland slips his tie back into his vest. "We've all fallen in love with your little town, sweetheart. Have you heard we've bought the cabin by the river?"

Tess grabs Rockland's arm, leaning into him. "I've already called my designer. We're going for woodsy elegance. You know—warm woods but break it up a little with white cabinets and—"

Rockland cuts her off with a pat on her hand. "You can show her the plans later, honey. I think she and Preston are...busy."

Preston runs his hand over the back of his neck. "Just looking for more...cups."

"Yes. Champagne flutes. Can never have enough of those," I say.

"Well, good luck!" Tess leaves us with a goodbye waggle of her fingers.

We're just about to duck into one of the empty rooms at the back of the hall when we catch Beau, looking like a damn GQ model in a white shirt and baby blue vest, his hair perfectly gelled, sneaking past the door…

And to my shock and delight, he's got a hot Bachman man on his tail.

"Matteo! Beau! How you doing, bros? I didn't know you two knew one another." Preston flashes his devilish grin, making Beau blush.

Matteo grabs my hand, bringing it to his lips and kissing it. "Jules. So lovely to meet you. Beau and Preston have told me so much about you. I'm happy to finally meet the woman who's stolen both their hearts."

Damn. This man is smooth. His dark eyes sparkle as he smiles. My heart does a little pitter-patter for my best friend. I like this guy.

"Pleasure is all mine. Are you both enjoying the party?" I ask, a light teasing in my tone.

The way they look at one another makes my heart soar. "Yeah. It's been pretty great," Beau says.

"Just wanted to find a quiet place to chat for a second. You know how the family is," Matteo says with a wink.

Preston's getting impatient. "See you guys. We've got plates to find."

"Cups," I correct him as he tugs me down the hall. I wave at the men over my shoulder. "Bye guys! So nice to meet you, Matteo."

Looks like Beau is softening up when it comes to his opinion of the Bachmans…

"Jesus. Is everyone using our place as their own private hook-up chalet?" Preston shakes his head.

"It's fun," I laugh. "The Bachmans are...spontaneous. That's something you've taught me."

"How about in here?" He opens the door of an old coat closet. *Our* coat closet, I have to remind myself, because we own this castle.

I'm still getting used to the idea.

He closes the door behind us, pulling up an old stool. "Sit here," he says.

I lean back on the stool. "Like this?" I ask.

"Just like that." He kneels down in front of me, dipping under my skirt. He pushes the layers of my fluffy dress upward, searching for my panties. He finds where he wants to be, nuzzling the gusset of my cotton panties with his nose. "You smell so good, baby."

His breath is hot against my sex, puffs of warm air travel through the fabric. My hands go to his hair.

"Mmm..." he presses against me. "You're my pretty little slut, aren't you? Letting me eat you out in the closet like this. You should be working but all you can think about is my tongue on you. Isn't that right?"

Truly, all I can think about is his tongue. "Yes. Please, kiss me."

"Kiss you where, baby?" He teases the seam of my sex over my panties. "I want you to say it."

Something that would have been hard for me before Preston comes to me easily now. "Kiss my pussy. Make your pretty little slut come. Hard."

He kisses and nips my inner thigh. "Damn girl. I love that dirty mouth of yours." He leaves my panties on, heating me with his hot breath and kisses. The feel of his touch and breath over the cotton gusset of the panties enhances my pleasure, making heat roll through my core.

He pulls the gusset to the side, teasing me by licking up either side of my slit, up and down, while fully avoiding the aching bud that wants his attention so badly. He runs a figure eight pattern, whipping around my clit.

More teasing. I moan, my fingers tugging at his hair. "Please baby. Lick it."

His fingers hook into the waistband of my panties. I lift my hips from the stool, letting him glide them down my legs and over my feet. He slips them in the pocket of his suit pants.

I lean back as he wraps his hand around the backs of my knees, parting my legs. His hot tongue dives between my thighs, entering me. It's warm and wet and having his tongue in me makes me feel shameful and sexy all at once.

But he's avoiding that oh-so-important area. I wriggle my hips against the stool, my fingers digging into the edge. I'm not above begging. "Please babe. Lick my clit."

He gives a chuckle at my impatience, the heat and rumble from his laughter only adding to my need. Finally, his tongue makes contact with my clit. "Yes! Just like that."

"I'm not letting you come."

"What?"

"Over that stool. Right now. I want to be inside you and I want to come inside that pretty little pussy of yours."

"Preston. You're killing me."

He grabs my hips, flipping me over. His hands are furiously flipping up my skirts. One hand presses into my lower back. The other makes quick work of his belt. He enters me, hard and fast. I'm so wet and ready for him but the hard thrust still burns as I stretch to take him.

He pulls the stool away, pushing me up against the wall. My palms go flat against the wood paneling. He strokes his way up my arm, grabbing my wrists and pinning them together in the strong circle of his thumb and forefinger. He holds my arms to the wall, his other hand grabbing my hip, bringing me back against him, hard.

He wraps his hand around my waist, tilting up my hips to dive deeper inside of me. My legs go numb, my knees start to shake. My body tightens around him. The climax shudders through me. I clench my muscles, holding him inside me as he comes. His arm wraps tighter, holding my ass against him as he gives a moan of pleasure.

"Come here, baby." He brings my hands down, wrapping both his arms around my waist as he kisses the curve of my neck. The heat from his mouth sends shivers down my spine. He holds me tighter, whispering in my ear. "I love you so much."

"I love you, too, babe." I turn over my shoulder, my lips searching for his, sealing our love with one, perfect kiss.

## 24

# Jules

Preston gets his wish. It's not after the hotel night, but a few weeks after we ditch the pills, I'm late. I feel a bit queasy, so I take one of the tests hidden in the bathroom cabinet. A minute later, a faint little pink plus sign pops up. Speechless, I walk out of the bathroom, test in one hand, paperwork in the other.

Where is Preston?

I find him in the living room, working on his laptop. "Look at this," I say, angling the test toward him.

His brow furrows as he stares at it. "A pregnancy test?"

I nod.

"What does this little sign mean?"

I can't answer him. There's a little life growing inside of me, and I haven't even done a pros and cons list to get there.

He takes the paper from my hand.

I just stare at that tiny pink sign, unable to believe he got his wish.

"Plus is pregnant." He's reading the paper, mumbling to himself. He stares at me, a massive smile stretching across his face. He jumps in the air, doing a victory cry. "Plus is pregnant!"

Tossing the paper down, he grabs my face in his hands and kisses me.

"You're pregnant." Preston takes me in his arms, lifting me from my chair. I wrap my arms around his neck as he spins me around the room. He stops, setting me back down. "Wait. You're pregnant. I shouldn't be spinning you like that."

"I'm okay," I say.

At least, I think I'm okay. My mind's never felt quite as cloudy as it does right now. A sense of joy and euphoria fill my chest yet it's almost impossible to process.

I am pregnant.

We're going to have a baby.

My hand goes to my flat belly, already knowing that I love this little baby inside me.

He cooks me dinner. Steamed baby carrots. Crispy roasted baby potatoes. Petite filets, and for dessert, mini cupcakes. I think my heart might burst as I lick the lemon frosting from the tiny little cake.

Preston is every bit as devoted as he said he would be. I've had to concede to his wishes on many occasions. No caffeine, no hard workouts, and no kinky sex. I've explained time and time again what's safe during pregnancy, but he insists it's missionary or gentle from the back, only until our baby is born.

The man is damn good at anything he puts his mind to in bed, so I'm not *too* put out.

I'M ONLY FOUR MONTHS ALONG WHEN PRESTON AND I ARE SEATED at our couples baby shower. It's earlier than one might normally have a shower, but I wanted everything prepared for baby Pippa to come, first, before I try to put together a wedding or we leave the country.

Preston agreed, knowing it was the only way I could relax on our honeymoon trip to Greece. The Beauties were more than happy to host.

The silver gown I wear hugs my curves, perfectly encasing my tiny bump. Preston glides up to me, rubbing a hand over the sparkly satin that covers my tummy. "My little snow globe," he says. Leaning down, he kisses the top of my belly.

A chorus of "awws," rise from women in the crowd. They can't get over how sweet Preston is with me and how devoted he is to the little girl growing inside me.

They say he's not even looked at another woman since he came back to Cedar Creek.

I don't flatter myself, there're plenty of beautiful women in the city. How can you not look? But he really does seem completely and utterly content with little ol' me. Even when I'm in my sweats and granny panties, curly hair having a mind of its own and the morning sickness making my face go green.

He tells me I'm beautiful. Rubs my feet and makes me peppermint tea.

"Here. Open mine next." Charlie leans forward, handing me a beautifully wrapped gift, the paper embossed with the coral and pink floral pattern she favors. There's a big pink and silver bow on top.

"It's too pretty to ruin." I carefully tug at the ends of the ribbon, trying to keep it intact for future use.

Inside the box, nestled in sparkly tissue paper, is a stack of gorgeous baby dresses, the fabrics all decorated with pretty floral patterns. Buried inside is a red leather Bachmans jewelry box.

"Aw, her first Bachmans," I say, flipping open the lid. "Oh, it's beautiful!"

I hold the little baby bracelet up for everyone to see. Our daughter's name is engraved in swirling letters on a little nameplate. We pass the precious piece of jewelry around.

The family is incredibly generous with gifts. They've taken care of the entire registry which had everything I needed for the nursery on it. And there are more clothes than she could possibly wear even if I changed her twice a day. Among the necessities, there're other gifts, handmade wall hangings with her name painted on them, an adorable teal and yellow quilt with little duckies on it, crocheted hats and mittens, and knitted blankets.

Those gifts are my favorites. The ones that people made, thinking of my sweet baby as they crafted them.

After the kitchen is cleaned up from the cake and appetizers, and the last teary-eyed Beauty leaves our door, I get right to putting the nursery together.

Preston looks at me with raised brows. "Right now? I haven't even cleaned up the wrapping paper yet."

I glance at the neatly folded stack of ribbons and gift bags and tissue I've saved. "Yes, please."

Lucky for me, where another man might have needed a nap after such an occasion, my Preston has boundless energy. An hour later, he's got all the presents carted up to the nursery and he's sitting cross-legged—the yoga we've been doing together has made him incredibly flexible—on the fluffy, pale-yellow rug, trying to figure out how to put the rocking bassinet together.

He's mumbling to himself something that sounds like, "Got myself a law degree but apparently you have to be an engineer to have a baby."

I just stand there, my hand on my tummy, taking in the finished nursery and my totally awesome, amazing husband-to-be.

I know times won't always be easy, but right now, my life is just about perfect. The castle is fully booked for the next six months. Beau is now my full-time event coordinator. My baby fashion social media account has gone viral.

My dad is settled and healthy and happy. I told my dad how angry I was that he did what he did to Preston. I told him everything Preston lost because of that one phone call he made in anger. My dad gave a heartfelt apology and now I feel like everything from the past is resolved.

I got a second chance with the first man I ever kissed.

In a few months, we'll be Mr. and Mrs., but I already have my happily ever after.

There's a knock on the door. Preston leaves his project. "Hang tight. I'll get that."

He returns, wrapping an arm around my shoulders. He hands me a buttery smooth envelope made of heavy cream-colored paper. My name is inked across the front in calligraphy.

"What's this?" I ask.

"I have no idea. Charlie just dropped it off."

I slip a manicured nail under the glue, opening the envelope. The inside is lined with gold. There's a small card inside, the cardstock embossed in gold letters.

*The Primetime Period Players would like to invite Jules Verduce to become a member of our esteemed club.*

"I can't believe it. They've asked me to join!"

Preston takes the card from me.

"Not these guys," he jokingly groans. "Does this mean more dress-up parties?"

"Yes! And this time, you're wearing tights." I laugh, taking the card from him and slip it back inside the envelope. I need to put this somewhere for safekeeping before my pregnancy brain kicks in. "Be right back."

I hurry to our bedroom, not wanting to be away from him even though he's just downstairs. I'm overwhelmed by the love I feel for Preston. It makes me realize there's something I've forgotten to do for him. Something I should have done a long time ago. I slip my phone from my pocket.

*#ALWAYSyourbaby*

Smiling, I slip my phone back in my pocket and go to the bottom of our closet. I pull out my wooden keepsake box. Inside is the globe from my mom, the napkin Preston left in my book with the message *You've never stopped tempting me,* my copy of *Pride and Prejudice*, my first ultrasound picture.

And four little Scrabble tiles from our game. The ones that spell out the greatest gift he's given me.

L O V E.

# EPILOGUE

## Rich

I'm standing at the altar, looking dapper in my black tux. I've got a single red rose in my lapel. My fiancée holds the other eleven in her bouquet. My best mate, Preston, is at my side, whispering nasty things in my ear trying to get me to laugh.

He thinks I'm nervous, but I'm not. He's been keeping the jokes going all afternoon, plying me with drinks to keep me loose. Sure, I've been a little on edge, but what man isn't on his wedding day?

It's cold feet, right? That icy knot in the pit of your stomach on your wedding day. It's just—what do they call it over here? Jitters? Wedding day jitters. That's all it is.

I stand at the altar, and I tell myself the feeling in my gut is one of excitement and not impending doom. But now, Preston's got his eyes back on that damn gold watch of his like every other person on this planet doesn't use their phone to tell time.

Would he just stop checking the damn time?

"Hey man, put that thing away," I say.

He looks out over the crowd. I follow his gaze. Hundreds of expectant Bachman faces. And they're all staring at me. I look at my groomsmen. One is stretching. One is yawning. One is bending his knees, shifting his weight from one foot to the other.

How long *have* we been standing here?

Where is she?

Father Patrick puts a hand on my shoulder. "Son. I hate to ask this but..." His voice trails off, leaving the question on everyone's mind hanging in the air.

"She's coming," I say. "She'll be here."

But as I say the words, I stop believing them.

She's been acting strangely the past few months. The Beauties told me not to worry, that it was just the way brides were. But as they said it, I could tell even they didn't believe it.

I kept thinking everything would work out. I just needed to get through the vows, to get that band on her finger, and we would start our lives together. Do all the things we planned.

But as I stand at this altar, sweat dampening my palms, I think about those plans. Did we make them together? Or was I the one doing all the planning?

I don't know.

I slip my empty hands into my pockets. Without my bride's hands to hold, I don't know what to do with them. I turn to Preston.

"She's not coming, is she?"

Preston runs a hand through his hair, leaving it standing on end. He shakes his head. "I don't think so, man. I'm sorry."

I stand there, in my anger and my shame, abandoned at the altar, all eyes on me.

I make myself a promise…

I'll never commit to another woman as long as I live.

Never again.

The NEXT BOOK: *Rich as Sin*

**He's rich as sin, and he wants to commit sins with me**

Fake relationship? I thought that was something that only happens in steamy romance novels.

But here he is, Richmond Bachman, as cocky as he is gorgeous, asking *me* to be his pretend date.

Did I mention he's a billionaire, tied to a secret society that runs New York City from behind closed doors?

Basically, my total opposite. I'm a nurse in the emergency room, working double shifts in glasses and scrubs. I haven't had a date since…okay, not going to admit that sad number out loud.

This massive man with an accent to make your panties melt came in needing help, and apparently, a date.

Would it be so bad to say *yes?* I mean, the poor guy recently got stood up literally at the altar. No wonder he's gone off dating.

Besides, I have something to gain from this charade. I need to let loose, have some fun, have a man in my bed before I forget how to. And who in their right mind is going to turn down a free trip to Greece? Hello—I've never even been out of the country.

I might be willing to play his game.

I'm just not willing to put my heart at stake.

Printed in Great Britain
by Amazon